A Note to Readers

Although the McMichael and Mikimoto families are fictional, the events they find themselves in are real. As America pulled out of the Great Depression, rumblings of war were all around. Japan was conquering countries in Asia. Germany, led by Adolf Hitler, was taking over nation after nation in Europe.

Many people in the United States didn't want to be in another war. But as time passed, attitudes toward going to war changed. Prejudice against Japanese-Americans also increased. Sometimes people vandalized Japanese-Americans' businesses and threatened their safety.

The good news was that during this time more people had jobs. Because of this, school attendance went up. There weren't special programs for extremely bright students. Instead, those children "skipped" grades. Some students finished school as much as two years early.

SISTERS IN TIME

Mandy
the Outsider

PRELUDE TO WORLD WAR 2

NORMA JEAN LUTZ

BARBOUR
PUBLISHING

In Memory of

Elizabeth Morgan Mattson: A grand lady!
To know her was to love her.

Cover design by Lookout Design Group, Inc.

Published by Barbour Publishing, Inc., P.O. Box 719, Uhrichsville, Ohio 44683
www.barbourbooks.com

Our mission is to publish and distribute inspirational products offering exceptional value and biblical encouragement to the masses.

 Member of the
Evangelical Christian
Publishers Association

Printed in the United States of America.
5 4 3 2 1

CONTENTS

CHAPTER 1

Labor Day Picnic

"Pic—nic. Pic—nic. We're going on a picnic. It didn't rain. It didn't rain. We're going on a picnic."

Amanda—"Mandy" to almost everyone—slipped farther down beneath the covers in an attempt to drown out the silly song that her sister Susan was singing. The bouncy five-year-old woke up bright and cheery nearly every morning. Today, Labor Day, she was more excited than usual.

"Come on, Mandy. Get up. Help me tie my shoes." Susan was standing close enough to Mandy's bed to make it jiggle. The jiggling was irritating, especially this early in the morning. Mandy lay still, pretending she was still asleep.

"Please, Mandy. I'm saying 'please.' You said 'please' is the magic word."

Susan now resorted to tugging on the bedcovers.

"Go away," Mandy muttered. "Get John to tie your shoes. Or Caroline."

"They're all downstairs. You're the last sleepyhead. Please hurry. Ben's been calling for me to come on."

Ben was Susan's twin and constant companion. The two of them were like a couple of bear cubs rollicking into mischief wherever they went. Both could be real pests at times. Especially when Mandy wanted to be left alone—which was now!

The bed bumped and creaked as Susan crawled up on it, placing both her feet close to Mandy's head. "Mama says if I walk downstairs with my shoes untied, I might fall."

Slowly, Mandy uncovered her head. As she did, the aromas of coffee and bacon accosted her sleepy senses. She sat up and found herself nose-to-nose with the grinning face of her curly-haired little sister. "Hi," Susan said, giving a little wave.

"How can you be so noisy this early?" Mandy tried unsuccessfully to stifle a big yawn.

"It's not early. Please hurry and tie my shoes. Please?"

Pushing back the covers, Mandy swung her feet over the side of the bed. "If I tie them, will you leave me alone for a while?"

Susan nodded and her glossy dark curls bobbed. "Sure I will. I'm going to help pack the picnic basket. Mama said I could."

Mandy felt a twinge of guilt for lying in bed while the rest of the family joined in the preparations. Pulling Susan's foot into her lap, she tied first one little brown oxford, then the other.

A picnic at the park on Labor Day hadn't gotten her vote. Mandy was hoping they would go back to the Fairfax Hotel, where they used to live. Not that she'd voiced her opinion. What good would it do when everyone else was so gung-ho on this picnic idea? She would have been terribly outnumbered.

"Your buttons are buttoned wrong." Mandy pointed to the front of Susan's playsuit.

Susan giggled as she looked down at her front. "They're all cockeyed, aren't they?"

"For sure. Here, let me fix them for you." Mandy unbuttoned and rebuttoned the playsuit. "You're all ready. Now scoot out

8

of here and leave me alone."

Susan looked up at Mandy. "You'll hurry, won't you? You don't want to make us late for the picnic, do you?"

Mandy wanted to ask how a person could be late for a picnic, but she didn't. "We won't be late," Mandy assured her. "I promise."

With that, Susan threw her arms around Mandy's neck and planted a wet kiss on her cheek. "Thank you, Mandy."

Mandy smiled in spite of her sour feelings. "You're welcome. Now get!"

Susan could be such a pain, but as soon as she was gone, their big bedroom suddenly took on a hollow, empty feeling. Mandy got up and began to straighten the chenille bedspread. The spread was patterned with pink rosebuds and a trim pink border on a mint green background. She'd helped Mama pick out the colors for the room. The vanity table with its large gold-frame mirror flanked the white bureau against the far wall. A ruffled mint-colored skirt hung on the vanity, and a matching tufted stool sat in front of it. Pink and mint green were repeated in the floral wallpaper and the priscilla curtains.

A person would have to be out of her mind to complain about such a lovely room. Yet, for some odd reason, Mandy still missed their old apartment at the Fairfax Hotel on Yesler Way. She knew it was silly, and she would never have admitted it to a soul, but she couldn't shake the feeling.

She reached down to pick up Susan's Shirley Temple doll with her mop of lifelike curls. In a copy of her older sister's *Silver Screen* magazine, she'd read about a Shirley Temple look-alike contest. Her sister Lora was an accountant for a shipping firm and could afford to purchase a copy of the magazine every week.

If they ever decided to enter Susan in a Shirley Temple look-alike contest, she'd surely win, with her curls and pouty lower lip. All they'd have to do is bleach her curls to a blond color and she'd be a shoo-in.

Mandy lay the doll on Susan's bed and padded barefoot across the golden hardwood floor to the bureau. Pulling out a pair of clean shorts and a shirt, she held them up and studied them. Both were faded from so many washings, having been passed from Lora down to Caroline and from Caroline to Mandy. In the McMichael family, hand-me-downs were *real* hand-me-downs.

There on the closet door hung Susan's new dress, all ready for her first day of kindergarten. Lucky Susan and Ben had new clothes for school. Mama had told the rest of them that hand-me-downs would have to do. They'd spent a great deal of money on furniture for the new house, so cash for new school clothes was not available.

On the table between their beds sat Susan's school supplies: scissors, paste, a pencil box, a box of eight sharp new Crayolas, two Laddie pencils, and one Big Chief ruled tablet. Each day, several times a day, Susan counted each piece and rearranged the stack. The kindergartner was thrilled about her first day of school. Mandy felt just the opposite. Going to school at Queen Anne Grammar was going to be much different from Bailey Gatzert School on Yesler Way. She dreaded it. Mark, Lora's boyfriend, called Queen Anne the snooty part of town. Since he was from Madrona Beach near Lake Washington, he should know. In high school, he'd played sports against teams from Queen Anne Hill.

Mandy dressed and sat down at the dressing table to brush her hair. With the rat-tail comb, she straightened her center part. Two red barrettes were fastened into place, one on each side, letting the waves fall loosely to her shoulders. Mama would probably tell her she should have braided her hair for the day, but she didn't feel like wearing little-kid pigtails today. Sharing a room with Susan made her feel enough like a baby. She didn't need pigtails to make it worse.

From the stairway, she could hear the voices coming up from the kitchen. They seemed so far away, as though everyone were in a distant country. When they lived at the Fairfax, they were only a few steps away from one another. Mama once said they lived on top of one another. But that was what Mandy loved most about their apartment. That closeness, plus Mrs. Mikimoto's wonderful Japanese cooking.

"Amanda!" John's voice called up the stairs. "Hey, slow-poke. The bacon's almost gone. You'd better hurry."

Bacon was Mandy's favorite part of breakfast. "You'd better save me a piece," she called back.

"Can't make guarantees for sleepyheads."

She grimaced at herself in the mirror. Her two-year-older brother could be so frustrating. "I'm coming!"

Mandy still didn't hurry as she went down the stairs, through the living room, and into the kitchen at the back of the house. Every room in their new house was as big as a cave. The kitchen was no exception. In fact, it was the spacious, light-splashed kitchen that caused Mandy's mom to say yes to buying this house. Over and over, Mandy had heard her mom say: "I want a kitchen big enough for all of us to sit down and eat together." That was asking a lot for a family with seven children, but at long last, Mama had her wish.

Nineteen-year-old Lora, looking lovely and poised as ever, stood at the sink washing pieces of chicken in preparation for frying them. Mother was cutting up the boiled potatoes for potato salad. Caroline had the silverware drawer open and was counting out the pieces to put into the wicker picnic basket.

"Well," Caroline said as Mandy came in, "it's about time. What a lazybones. You should be helping out." At fourteen, Caroline had begun to sound more like a mother than a sister.

"It's supposed to be a holiday," Mandy protested feebly. All this busyness made the guilt-pricks sharper than before.

Mother took one look at her and said, "Mandy, you should have braided your hair. It's a picnic."

"I want to wear it down." She filled her plate with the last of the bacon from the skillet on the stove, then took a bottle of milk from the fridge to fix a bowl of Wheaties.

Mama made them take turns getting their favorite cereal. Wheaties was John's favorite because it sported a picture of Jack Armstrong, the All-American boy. John never missed an episode of Jack Armstrong on the radio. He'd even sent off for the Jack Armstrong whistle ring, along with the secret whistle code. He and Baiko and Dayu Mikimoto used to play with their whistle rings together when they lived on Yesler Way. She hadn't seen the ring since they moved.

Pouring a glass of milk, Mandy stirred in heaping spoonfuls of Ovaltine to make the good-tasting chocolate-flavored drink. She, on the other hand, liked to listen to Little Orphan Annie's radio show. Orphan Annie loved to say:

For extra pep 'n' flavor keen,
Drink chocolate-flavored Ovaltine!

Spooning up the soggy Wheaties, Mandy gazed out the windows to see the twins taking turns riding piggyback on Peter around the yard. Susan's squeals of laughter floated in through the open window. Mandy could remember when her older brother used to give her piggyback rides, but she was too big for that sort of thing now. Sometimes she wished time could stand still. Change was such a scary thing—especially when so many changes came at once.

Yesterday, when they arrived home from church, Dad switched on the console radio in the living room in time to hear the news that Britain had declared war against Germany. Although Dad, Peter, and Lora's boyfriend, Mark, talked on and on about the war, Mandy tried her best to ignore them. She didn't want to hear about the fighting and bombing and killing. In one direction, Japan was waging war on China, and in the other direction, Nazi Germany was attempting to take over Europe. When Mandy heard adults talking, they were asking, "Will the U.S. be next?"

The question that haunted Mandy was, if the U.S. went to war, would her beloved Peter have to go? She couldn't bear the thought. Peter was the only one in the family who loved books as much as she did. He seemed to understand when she preferred to have her nose buried in a good book rather than be doing her chores.

Now the twins were playing tag, and Peter was helping Dad clean out the trunk of their new burgundy-colored DeSoto.

Long-legged and slender, Peter stood a few inches taller than Dad. With his dark hair and clear blue eyes, Peter was about the most handsome boy in the world, Mandy thought. The twins kept running up behind him as though to scare him, and he joined in their fun, even as he was helping Dad. That was just like Peter.

Hurriedly, Mandy finished the Wheaties, rinsed her dish and tumbler, and joined in the picnic preparations. Mother set her to cutting the carrot and celery sticks and wrapping them in squares of waxed paper.

Just as the golden-brown chicken was ready to be lifted from the skillets, Mandy heard Lora give a little gasp. Only one thing these days took Lora's breath away, and that was Mark Johnson. Sure enough, in a moment they all heard the rattle of his old black Ford pulling into the drive. The thing shimmied and shook so that Mandy thought the fenders might fall off.

Lora dropped the towel in her hands and ran out the back door, letting the screen door slam just like Mama daily told all the rest of them not to do. Mandy guessed rules could be broken when you were grown up and had fallen in love.

"Mama!" Caroline cried out as she gaped out the window. "He's kissing her right in front of the whole world."

"Caroline McMichael, you get away from that window this minute," Mama ordered.

But Caroline ignored her. "Why should I miss out on what all the neighbors are seeing?" All dreamy-eyed, she added, "Mmm. It's so, so romantic. Almost like Rhett and Scarlett in *Gone with the Wind.*" Turning from the window, she said, "Mama, do you think I'll ever have a man love me like Mark loves Lora?"

Just then, John popped in the back door and heard the question. Ruffling Caroline's hair, he said, "Love you? You must be joking. Who'd wanna fall in love with a girl who can beat them at baseball, touch football, and marbles?"

Caroline shoved him away. "Oh, go away. Nobody asked for your feeble opinion."

John stumbled and acted like he was falling. "Ah, she got me. The tough woman got me. I'm dying. Argh! Gasp! Dying!"

Mandy laughed at their antics, but Mama said for them to stop it that instant. "Let's use our energy to get this food packed."

"Oh, yeah." John grinned sheepishly. "That's why I came in. Dad wants to know what's ready to be loaded."

Within the hour, both Mark's old Ford and the McMichaels' DeSoto were loaded, and they were off to Kinnear Park. Mandy had even slipped in her newest Nancy Drew mystery without anyone noticing. With any luck, she'd have the whole thing read before the day was out.

John and Ben chose to ride with Mark and Lora. That left more room in the backseat of the DeSoto. Dad was so proud of their car. He'd bought it from a fellow worker at the Boeing plant just a week or two earlier. Her father had vacuumed it, washed and waxed it, and put on new tires.

But as with the new house, Mandy felt disoriented—as though she were riding along in someone else's body in someone else's place. Her place was in their old apartment at the Fairfax Hotel on Yesler Way. And Baiko and Dayu were there waiting for her and John to come outside and play.

CHAPTER 2

The Golden Ring

The shady park wasn't far from their house, and Dad teased them about being softies—riding in the car when they could walk. But Mama said she'd like to see him walk and carry all the baskets of food, plus the blankets.

"Now, Nora," he said, patting her arm, "we did it when we were kids."

Mama only smiled. Mandy figured Mama knew Dad loved driving his new car and that he wasn't really protesting at all.

The park was crowded. They drove through the winding, shady drives looking for empty picnic tables. Finally, Dad said, "Aw, who cares about tables? We'll spread the blankets under the shade trees." He motioned to Mark, who was following close behind, to park along the road, and they all piled out.

Mandy had to admit nothing was as lovely as Kinnear Park down near the waterfront. The soft carpet of grass smelled sweet and clean as she spread a blanket over it. The food was quickly spread before them, and after Dad said grace, they dug in. The twins were finished eating and ready to play almost before the others had started. Peter said the two of them moved like greased lightning.

Since everyone was stuffed, they voted to wait until later in the afternoon to cut Mama's layered chocolate cake. Peter took the twins off for a walk on the path through the woods, and John and Caroline challenged Lora and Mark to a game of badminton. Peter never asked if Mandy wanted to come along on the walk, and the foursome never asked if she wanted to play. Nine, Mandy decided, was a nothing age to be.

As Mandy went to the car to retrieve her book, she heard Mama call out, "Don't overdo now, John. If you get winded, please stop right away."

John continued running around, knocking the feathered shuttlecock over the net as though she'd never said a word. Mandy knew John was embarrassed half to death when Mama called out to him like that.

Ever since John's last frightening coughing attack, Mama seemed to hover over him—more so even than with the twins. But then, Mandy, too, was terrified when John coughed and coughed and coughed and couldn't get his breath.

Taking her book, Mandy walked a ways into the woods until she found a nice place to lean against a tree and read. Overhead, the birds sang their hearts out, and in the distance, the lonely ship whistles sounded in Elliott Bay.

She was nearly halfway through the book when she heard voices and footsteps along the path. Thinking it was Peter and the twins, she jumped up to hide behind the tree. She held her breath, waiting to leap out and scare them.

But it wasn't Peter and the twins. Instead, it was four girls who all looked to be about Mandy's age or a little older. Quickly, she pulled her head back and pressed closer to the rough bark of the tree.

"And we can call our group the Golden Ring," one of the girls was saying.

"Oh, Elizabeth," said another. "That's a wonderful name. How'd you ever think of it?"

"You know the answer to that, Jane. I'm smart, that's all."

The girls giggled at the comment. As they passed by the tree, Mandy peered around at them. All four wore neatly cuffed shorts with blouses that matched. Their black-and-white saddle oxfords showed no scuffs on the white parts, and their anklets were neatly turned down.

"We'll be able to do most anything we want all during fourth grade," said the girl with long, honey-colored hair, the one named Elizabeth. "Old deaf and blind Mrs. Crowley won't see a thing."

"Dow–dy Mrs. Crowley," said another. The other three joined in the chant, singing, "Dow–dy Mrs. Crowley," then burst into giggles.

Mandy stared at the foursome as their voices faded into the distance. She glanced down at her faded play clothes and scuffed oxfords. Deaf and blind Mrs. Crowley? Now she dreaded the first day of school more than ever.

Just as Mandy suspected, Susan was up at the crack of dawn the next morning, singing her little songs about going to school. *You would think it's Christmas or something,* Mandy thought as she turned over and tried to ignore the noise. It couldn't be anywhere near time to get up.

Lucky Lora. She got to go to work at Gaylor Shipping each

day. None of this stuff about being the new kid at a new school, and all the worry that went with it, for her. Half-awake, Mandy dreamed of four girls surrounded by a glowing, halolike golden ring. They walked along in a fuzzy cloud where saddle oxfords were never scuffed.

"Mandy! Mandy, are you awake?" It was Mama's voice from out in the hall.

"She's awake," Susan said with a giggle. "But she's acting like she's not."

"Everybody up," Mama said. "We don't want anyone to be late on the first day of school."

Mandy groaned. When she had attended Bailey Gatzert, no one had had to tell her to get up. She loved going to school with all the kids in the neighborhood.

"Button me, please, Mandy." *Jiggle, jiggle* went the bed. "And tie my sash, too, please."

Mandy heaved a sigh and threw back the covers. This was silly. The little sister should be the one who was frightened of going to school, not the big sister. Dutifully, she buttoned the back of Susan's cute little print dress and tied the sash in a bow, making sure the ends hung down just right.

"Thank you," Susan said primly. She picked up her armload of school supplies and went out the door. Mandy watched her, wondering what Susan would do for the next three-quarters of an hour before it was time to leave the house.

Standing in front of her closet, Mandy closed her eyes and grabbed a dress. It didn't really matter which one. She was thankful that John was still in grade school with her. Walking into the school with him would make things a little easier.

Mama asked the twins if they wanted her to come along on their first day. They said no. *She's asking the wrong ones,* Mandy thought as she pulled on her brown school shoes and tied the laces. She was the one who felt like holding Mama's hand today.

Peter took the bus to the high school, and the junior high Caroline attended was in the opposite direction from Queen Anne Grammar. Mandy marveled that Caroline didn't seem a bit afraid. John was the same way. In fact, John had gone out looking for boys his age the very day they moved in. "If we'd come earlier in the summer, I'd have found a few," he said after a fruitless search.

Dad said they lived on the edges of the Queen Anne Hill community and mostly older folk lived in their immediate neighborhood. "You'll make friends at school," Dad had promised.

When they arrived at the playground, the first thing Mandy noticed was that all the faces looked alike. Her old school, located smack in the middle of the international district, had kids of all races and all nationalities. Dad called it the melting pot of the city. No one was really like anyone else, yet everyone was accepted. As the white faces stared at this new family coming into their world, Mandy wished she had taken time to appreciate her old school more when she was there.

Queen Anne Grammar was a buff brick building, rather new looking, long and low and spread out. It was nothing like stocky, two-story, old worn-out Bailey Gatzert. The chain-link fence here was sturdy and in good repair. The teeter-totters, jungle gym, swings, and slippery slide looked newer as well.

Silently, the four McMichael children climbed the front steps. The twins were a bit more subdued, and they moved closer to one another. How Mandy wished she had someone to hang close to all day.

John stepped ahead to open the front door, and they filed into the front hallway, which was lined with trophy cases. Filled-up trophy cases. Mandy wondered if this school had won every prize in every school event in the city.

Though they hadn't discussed it, Mandy thought John was going to go with her to take the twins to the kindergarten room. She was wrong. After they stopped in the office to learn where their rooms were located, John said, "You go on and take the twins to their room. I'll see you at lunch."

"I'm going home for lunch, remember?"

"I'll probably see you at recess then." And he was gone. The traitor.

Though most of the students were out on the playground, a few were in the hall, probably looking for their classrooms as well.

The school had three wings—A, B, and C, the lady in the office explained. Mandy took the twins down the long hallway of C wing to the very end. There the friendly kindergarten teacher, looking not much older than Lora, met them at the door.

"Hello, there," she said. "I'm Miss Applegate."

Ben giggled. Leaning over to Susan, he said, "Do we bring apples to Miss Applegate?" Then Susan giggled.

"Some students do," said Miss Applegate. "You must be the McMichael twins."

Susan lifted up her armload of stuff. "I have all my supplies right here. I'm ready for school."

"I see you are," Miss Applegate answered. Then she smiled at Mandy as though they had a secret together. "Come in, children, and I'll show you where to put your things away."

The twins never looked back. The teacher glanced back at Mandy, mouthed "Thank you," and turned away as well.

Now Mandy had to walk all the way back down C wing by herself. The fourth-grade room was in A wing on the opposite side of the office.

As she approached the main hall again, a girl came running around the corner and nearly slammed into her. Mandy would have recognized that flowing honey-colored hair anywhere. It was the girl she'd seen in the park.

After catching her balance, the girl said, "Hey, you need to watch where you're going."

Mandy hadn't been the one who was running, but she said nothing. She just kept on walking.

When she found the fourth-grade room, she quickly discovered why the girls at the park said "Dowdy Mrs. Crowley." Stepping inside, she saw an elderly woman standing at the blackboard, writing on the board with a shaky hand that was etched with wrinkles and blue veins. Her close-cropped thin gray hair allowed bits of pink scalp to show through. *Why does the school board allow such an old woman to continue teaching?* Mandy wondered.

She stood at the door a moment. No other students were in the room. Mandy hoped that meant she could choose where she wanted to sit. She cleared her throat in hopes of being noticed. The teacher didn't seem to hear. Mandy stepped farther into the room, hoping her footsteps would attract attention. Nothing. Mrs. Crowley kept on writing. She wrote a Scripture verse, then added the date, September 5, 1939, and her name, Mrs. Violet Crowley.

Clearing her throat again, Mandy took two more steps and said, "Excuse me, please."

"What?" Mrs. Crowley turned about. "Well, well. A new student. You aren't supposed to be in here yet. All the children are out on the playground."

Didn't this teacher even want to know who she was? "May I put my things down?" Mandy's arms were getting tired of holding the books and supplies.

Mrs. Crowley waved a veined hand, covered lightly with chalk dust. "Put them anywhere and get on out to the playground, child."

"Yes, ma'am." Mandy didn't hurry as she walked around the room looking for an empty desk. She found one midway in the row nearest the windows. After she set her things down, she walked slowly to the main hall and out the front door. Just as she opened the door, a loud electric buzzer sounded, and she nearly jumped out of her skin.

"Get in line," came a voice from behind her.

The students were lining up by grades, but Mandy had no idea which grade was which until she saw the girl with the honey-colored hair. She went to the end of that line.

As she walked with the others up the stairs and down the hall, she noticed a girl in line ahead of her who was nearly as tall as a sixth-grader. Not just tall, but big-boned. And when she walked, she limped along with a strange, rolling gait. The special-built shoes, one with a sole thicker than the other, were uglier than Mandy's brown oxfords. Much uglier. The girl's hair looked like it hadn't seen a comb in days. Mandy tried not to stare.

After Mrs. Crowley brought her class to order—which took a little while—she called the roll. That's when Mandy learned that the girl with the limp was Helga Gottman. And the girl with the pretty honey-colored hair was Elizabeth Barrington.

When Mandy's name was called, she answered so softly Mrs. Crowley didn't hear. Looking up, she scanned the room, glaring over her small reading glasses as though she had two sets of eyes. "Mandy McMichael?" she said, raising her voice. "Speak loudly and clearly, please."

Some of the kids snickered.

Blushing, Mandy answered in a louder voice. "Here." They snickered again.

After the morning Scripture reading, prayer, flag salute, and singing of the national anthem, Mrs. Crowley reviewed who had which textbooks and workbooks and which ones still needed to be ordered. When those details were out of the way, she asked the students to take out their math books.

By this time, Mandy had the four girls from the Golden Ring figured out. Elizabeth, of course, and a dark-haired girl named Jane Stevens. The other two were Renee Ford and Lily Madison. The four were sitting in a close little group just one row over from Mandy. After they made a joke, the girls would hook little fingers, like a secret handshake. Mandy saw no other girls hooking little fingers except the four in the Golden Ring.

They whispered during class time, but Mrs. Crowley didn't

seem to mind. Or perhaps she couldn't hear.

"How many of you know your multiplication tables by heart?" Mrs. Crowley asked. "All the way up to twelve."

Mandy raised her hand without thinking. She should have waited a moment. Hers was the only hand up. Unless there was one behind her. . .

"Only one student?" Mrs. Crowley asked. Her tone was one of shock.

Mandy put her hand down quickly, feeling the cold stares around her. The four in the Golden Ring were twittering softly. Was there something wrong with knowing all the times tables by heart?

Lora had helped her with fractions and decimals last winter, but when Mrs. Crowley asked who knew about fractions and decimals, Mandy wouldn't have raised her hand for anything.

The morning dragged on until it was time for recess. At least Mandy thought it was supposed to be recess. Instead, they were to report to the gymnasium for a physical education class, as Mrs. Crowley called it. Students in junior high schools and high schools had phys-ed classes, but a grammar school? This didn't sound like much fun to Mandy.

The phys-ed teacher's name was Miss Bowen. Miss Bowen carried an important-looking clipboard and had a big voice that filled the entire gymnasium. Her booming voice bounced against the high ceilings and came down on their heads like a driving rain. Dressed in navy blue shorts, a white blouse, and trim white sneakers, Miss Bowen shouted, "All right, everybody. File in and sit on the floor in neat, straight rows."

Helga Gottman's special shoes made an awful clomping

sound as she made her roll-step right up to the front, right under Miss Bowen's nose.

"Wouldn't you know? It's tottery, doddery Gottman," hissed a voice down the row from Mandy. Snickers followed. It was Elizabeth and her adoring followers.

"Quiet!" came Miss Bowen's booming voice. "I'll be the only one talking in this room."

Elizabeth whispered, "You call that talking?" Again the girls snickered.

Mandy wondered if the girls did anything besides snicker at other people. She was already beginning to dislike Queen Anne Grammar—most intensely.

When Miss Bowen described the year's plan for phys-ed class—the gym suits they had to wear, showers they had to take, laps they had to run, and sports they all must be involved in—Mandy was ready to go back to Yesler Way and live with the Mikimotos!

CHAPTER 3

Library Day

The dramatic theme music for the *Romance of Helen Trent* was playing on the radio when Mandy and the twins walked into the kitchen for lunch. After *Helen Trent* would come *Our Gal Sunday*. All through the summer as she helped Mama around the house, Mandy listened to the soap operas to see what would happen the next day. The make-believe world always had many problems, but there were always answers.

Her favorite was *Just Plain Bill*, "a story about people who might be your own next-door neighbors," the announcer told listeners. But Mandy couldn't think of anyone she knew who were like the people on the radio shows.

"To get your teeth doubly clean," the radio announcer was saying as Mandy washed up at the kitchen sink, "use Dr. Lyons' Tooth Powder. Dr. Lyons removes film and surface stain with its remarkable cleaning power."

Peter said once that if they believed everything the radio advertisers said, they'd have to use fifteen different tooth powders and twenty different kinds of laundry soap.

The wringer washer was sitting in the middle of the kitchen chugging away, giving off the clean, soapy aromas of wash day. Mandy would have been more than happy to stay home and help hang the laundry out on the clothesline. Mama turned off the washing machine long enough to serve up their bowls of tomato soup and cheese sandwiches, then turned back to guiding the clothes carefully through the wringer into the rinse water.

Between doing the laundry and listening to the twins raving about their wonderful first day of kindergarten, Mama hardly had a moment to look at Mandy. How Mandy wished Mama would ask her how the day was for her. But even if she had, Mandy wasn't sure she would have been able to answer. After all, she didn't want to be a whiny baby. That's what John called her when she complained.

She did tell her mother about needing a gym suit. Mama looked up from the steamy laundry and pushed a lock of hair out of her face. "Really? I don't remember seeing that on the list."

"Whether it was or not, I still need it. We have physical education class every morning."

Mama just nodded. "I suppose I can run downtown after the wash is hung out and the twins finish their naps." She went back to her work. *Ma Perkins* was coming on just as Mandy left to go back to school.

The afternoon was worse than the morning, only without Miss Bowen's shouting. During geography, Mandy forgot for a moment where she was, and when Mrs. Crowley asked a question, her hand shot up before she could stop it.

"Show-off," she heard someone whisper. Unlike Miss Bowen in the noisy gymnasium, Mrs. Crowley heard none of the whispering.

The afternoon hours dragged slowly by. At recess, Mandy

kept to herself, which was more than easy since no one paid a bit of attention to her. She didn't know which was worse, being ignored or being tormented like Helga. Neither she nor Helga seemed to fit in anywhere. The only difference was Helga fought back. For Mandy, it was safer to retreat.

John, on the other hand, was involved in a rousing, noisy game of baseball with all the other fellows. He was an outfielder, but at least he was in the game. Maybe it was easier being a boy. Tomorrow she'd bring a book to read at recess time.

"It's your week to do the ironing," Caroline said to Mandy as they set the table for supper that evening.

"I know, I know." Mandy certainly didn't need Caroline to tell her what jobs belonged to whom since Mama kept the job schedule posted on the corkboard beside the fridge. Anyone with eyes could see it. Actually, it was Lora and Mandy's week. One week Mama and Caroline took on the bushel basket of ironing, the next week Lora and Mandy took it. But Caroline hadn't mentioned Lora.

The familiar chug of Mark's Ford sounded outside as he brought Lora home from work. He worked as a longshoreman for Gaylor Shipping.

"Will Mark be staying for supper?" Mandy asked, wondering if they needed another place setting.

"Well, we can't know that until Lora comes in, now can we?" Caroline snapped.

"I just asked," Mandy said softly. What had she done to make her older sister so snippity?

When a smiling Lora came through the door and they heard the sound of the Ford backing out of the drive, Caroline said to Mandy, "There's your answer." Mandy ignored her.

Lora was glowing, as she always was after she'd been with Mark for any length of time. "Hi, everyone," she said as she breezed through the kitchen. "I'll get changed and be right down to help."

Mandy watched her older sister with eyes of envy. She tried, without much success, to imagine what it would be like to belong to someone special like Lora belonged to her Mark.

Peter would be arriving shortly from his after-school job of pumping gas at the Tydol filling station. He always came home with grease up to his elbows and grimy fingernails. Mandy never thought he really liked doing such a messy job. But as he said, "It's a job."

Dad, on the other hand, wouldn't be there for supper. Since Dad had been working overtime at Boeing, Mama kept his supper warm in the oven.

All through supper the conversation danced about from one young McMichael to the next, as they told the happenings of their first day of school. Mandy said very little. Presently, Peter happened to look over at her.

"You're awful quiet tonight, little sis." He stretched his long leg under the table and tapped her ankle with his foot. "Everything okay?"

She nodded. "Everything's okay." She forced her face to smile.

"I know what Mandy's problem is," John put in.

Mandy held her breath, hoping he wouldn't tell how she was off by herself at recess.

"What is it, John?" Susan asked, her face screwed up in a frown. "What's Mandy's problem?"

"Her class hasn't had library day yet. Ours is tomorrow."

"Library day?" Mandy was sure she hadn't heard Mrs. Crowley say anything about a library day.

Lora laughed. "Well, we all know everything's all right in Mandy's world once she locates the library."

"Hey, now," Peter countered. "Nothing wrong with loving a good book. Right, Mandy?"

"Right, Peter." It felt good to hear Peter talk as though the two of them had a special secret. But the feeling was fleeting as the conversation sailed right on. Well, at least she knew there was going to be a library day at Queen Anne School. Things were looking up—even if just a smidgen.

The girls in the Golden Ring chose the time in the locker room to gang up on Helga. The more they made fun of her, the louder Helga talked back to them. The louder she talked back in her raspy voice, the more they laughed at her.

"Move your stuff, Clubfoot," one of the Golden Ring said to her, pushing her clothes off the bench and onto the damp floor.

"You better cut that out right now," Helga answered in her thick voice. "And I mean it, too."

"You better cut that out right now," another girl mocked.

Mandy wished someone would make them be quiet. But she knew she wasn't the one to do it. Secretly, she was glad it was Helga and not her they were picking on. Yet even that thought ate at her midsection.

In gym class, the barking Miss Bowen made them run laps around the gymnasium, and Helga had to run right along with all the rest. Of course, she couldn't keep up in her clumsy, rolling gait. Some of the faster runners passed her several times. Mandy had to give the girl credit. In spite of the rude remarks, Helga kept on huffing and puffing around the gym.

Mandy learned that Friday was library day for the fourth-graders. She could hardly wait. Friday was a welcome day anyway since it meant she'd have two whole days in a row away from Queen Anne School, but now it also meant she'd have fresh new books to read.

The library was located down the stairs just beneath the front office. It was more beautiful than Mandy could ever have imagined. Large, roomy, well lighted, and best of all, well stocked. Afternoon sunshine streamed in through the high windows, laying golden patches on the glossy hardwood floor.

"May I have your attention, fourth-graders," came a high melodic voice. The murmuring and whispering stopped as a small, brown-eyed young lady stepped into the center of their group.

"My name is Miss LaFayette, and I'm your new librarian. Welcome to your library day." She went over the rules of checking books out for only one week and warned them to return books and not lose them. "If you lose a library book, we may have to suspend your borrowing privileges."

"Say," whispered a boy standing directly behind Mandy. "What a great reason to lose a book. I don't want to borrow any anyway. I hate reading."

Hate reading? Mandy couldn't imagine such a thing. As the pretty librarian continued to talk, Mandy began to scan the shelves nearest her. She saw fantasies, adventure stories, mysteries, and plenty of biographies of famous people. As soon as Miss LaFayette stopped talking, Mandy grabbed a couple of books and went to the reading area off in the corner. They had a full hour of library time.

When only about fifteen minutes were left, Mandy chose five books from the shelves and stood in line to check them out. When she stepped up to Miss LaFayette's desk, the librarian looked up at Mandy, her soft brown eyes wide. "Five books?"

Mandy nodded, feeling her face grow red. "Is that all right?"

"There's a limit of two per week. I mentioned it when I was explaining the rules a moment ago."

That must have been the moment when Mandy stopped listening and started studying book titles. "I'm sorry. I must have missed that part. But I'll have two books read by Monday."

Miss LaFayette chuckled. "I guess you like to read."

Mandy nodded. She wished she could tell her just how much she loved books, but there were too many ears nearby.

"Choose two for this time," Miss LaFayette directed. "If you continue to bring your books back on time, we'll let you check out more."

Reluctantly, Mandy chose two out of the five and turned to place the other three back on the shelves. As she did, she saw the girls in the Golden Ring hovering near the end of the line of fourth-graders. They were one row away from where Mandy had to return one of the biographies.

Elizabeth's loud singsong whisper came floating over the

bookshelf, "Oh please, Miss LaFayette. Please let me check out fifty books. I promise I'll have them all back by next week."

"Oh, you silly, silly girl," answered another mocking voice, "just take the whole library home with you. Why, we don't mind at all."

Snickers and giggles followed as though that were the funniest joke of the century. Her face burning, Mandy slipped the books back into their places and hurried back to the classroom. Those girls were probably hooking little fingers as they laughed.

As if things couldn't get any worse, later that afternoon, Mrs. Crowley handed back their spelling tests. Laying Mandy's paper on her desk, the teacher announced to the whole world, "First spelling test of the year, and Mandy McMichael received the only perfect score in the entire class. Fine job, Mandy. Fine job!" And the old lady actually patted Mandy's shoulder with her thin vein-lined hand.

Mandy shuddered inwardly and wanted to drop through the floor. Sure enough, when school was dismissed and the students filled the halls, she heard the mocking voices behind her, "Fine job, Mandy Einstein. Fine, fine job. We're so, so proud of you."

Mandy was sure she was going to die right there in the front hall of Queen Anne School!

CHAPTER 4

Mephibosheth

On Saturday night, Lora had a date with Mark, and Peter was working at the filling station. But the rest of the family planned to spend the evening with the Mikimotos. Mandy was pleased. A hurricane could be blowing Seattle off the map, yet inside the Mikimoto home it would still be serene and peaceful. Mr. and Mrs. Mikimoto simply wouldn't allow it to be any other way.

The Mikimoto children had been their playmates all the years the McMichaels had lived at the Fairfax. Baiko and Dayu not only played games with John, but they always included Mandy as well. And even though their older sister, Hideko, was Caroline's age, she never treated Mandy like a little kid. In fact, Mandy had never known a left-out feeling while she lived there.

Even Caroline seemed happy that they were going back for a visit. As they drove through downtown Seattle in the DeSoto, Caroline wondered aloud if Hideko would still be her friend.

Mother tried to calm her fears. "Don't worry, Caroline," she said, "you know how loyal the Japanese are. Hideko will never stop being your friend."

Dad parked on the street in front of the large, red-brick building. The sidewalk was flanked by almost every business imaginable. A friendly Italian restaurant stood next to the stairs that led to the front entrance of the hotel. Farther down the street was the secondhand store where Mama and Dad purchased many of their clothes when they first arrived in Seattle. Next came the barbershop, and on the corner was the cigar shop.

Down the other way was the union office with the filthy fly-specked front windows, the Chinese laundry, and the burlesque house, where they were forbidden to even peek inside one of the painted windows. Mandy marveled that everything was just as they'd left it. Even the heavy aromas from the Italian restaurant were exactly the same.

As soon as Mrs. Mikimoto politely answered the door and ushered them in, Mandy could smell the aroma of rice balls with pickled plums in the center. Her favorite. She was the only one of the McMichaels who loved the bright red salty plums as much as the Mikimotos.

Bowing and offering polite greetings, Mr. and Mrs. Mikimoto led the McMichaels into the dining room, where they took their seats. The small dining room was adjacent to Mrs. Mikimoto's kitchen. Everything in the hotel was compact and orderly.

Mother had brought along two freshly baked pies, which Mrs. Mikimoto insisted she shouldn't have done. But Mrs. Mikimoto graciously took them and set them on the kitchen counter. Mama had always said she hoped the Mikimotos' good manners would rub off on all her children.

As they ate, Dad and Mr. Mikimoto talked about the rumors of war with Japan. "It is as though the madness of Hitler has touched the militarists of Japan," said Mr. Mikimoto, shaking his head gravely. "And whatever madness they perform, those around here blame us."

John lay down his red-lacquered chopsticks. "No one can blame you for what's happening clear across the Pacific, can they? Why, that would be like blaming every German-American for what Hitler is doing."

"They can," said Mr. Mikimoto, "and they do." He paused while his wife brought a fresh pot of tea to the table. "If there is war between Japan and this country, my wife and I will be considered enemy aliens."

Mandy nearly choked on her pickled plum. "But Mr. Mikimoto, it's not your fault that you're not a citizen," she protested. "The law won't let you. Isn't that right?"

Mr. Mikimoto gave a polite nod in her direction. "Quite so, Mandy. We are prevented from becoming citizens by the immigration law passed way back in 1924. Perhaps because people are afraid of us. I do not know."

Mandy couldn't imagine anyone being afraid of this kind and gentle man.

"What's an alien?" Ben wanted to know.

Ignoring his little brother, John said, "You want to become citizens and can't, yet you're considered aliens because you're not citizens. Doesn't make much sense to me."

"Thank goodness we're all citizens," Baiko said, waving his hand to include himself, his brother, and his sister.

"That's right," Dayu echoed. "I'm no alien."

"What's an alien?" Ben asked again.

"Someone who's not a citizen of a country," Mother answered him.

"What's a citizen?" Susan asked.

Dad chuckled. "Five years old—the question-asking age." Turning to the twins, he said, "I'll explain it when we get home tonight."

"Enough of all this depressing talk," Hideko said. "Mama-san, may we be excused so I can show our guests the new addition to the family?"

"What new addition?" John asked.

"You'll see," Hideko said, her almond eyes squinting as she smiled.

"What?" Dad teased her. "No apple pie?"

"We can have pie later," Dayu said as he scooted back his chair. "May we go, Mama-san?"

"You may," Mrs. Mikimoto said in her quiet voice.

As they filed out into the apartment hallway, John asked, "What do you mean about a new addition? You have new people coming into the hotel almost every day."

"Not a tenant, silly," Baiko said, punching John on the shoulder.

"To my room," Hideko ordered.

"Wait for me," Susan called as she brought up the rear. Mandy waited for her, then picked up her little sister in her arms.

The children followed after Hideko, trying to keep their giggles down so as not to disturb other guests.

Hideko opened the door to her cozy little bedroom, which was lined with shelves full of books and exquisite handmade Japanese dolls in silk kimonos. There, lying in the center of her bed, was a half-grown gray and white kitten.

"Ohh," Susan breathed. "A kitty-cat."

"I thought your mama said she wouldn't allow you to have

pets," Caroline said as she sat down beside the kitten and began petting it.

Hideko laughed. "We kept pestering her, and she finally gave in. Right, boys?"

"Right," Dayu said with a big smile. "And Mittens has already earned her keep. She killed two mice in one week."

"And that convinced Father right away to let us keep her," Hideko said. "She was a stray out in the alley, and we fed her for a while before asking if we could keep her."

Dayu crawled over the foot of the bed and sat down in the corner. "Mama said that if her grandfather were alive and were here, he'd call the cat a goblin."

"A goblin?" Caroline asked, petting the kitten. "How could anyone call this cute little thing a goblin?"

Mandy pushed in and sat Susan down on the bed so they could pet the kitten, too. Its fur was silky and felt soft and clean. "She doesn't look like an alley cat." Mandy felt the rumble of purring beneath her fingertips.

"You can bet Hideko has already given her a couple baths," Dayu said.

"She may hate water," Hideko said, "but it's easier to get *her* into the tub than either of my two brothers."

Her joke set them all to laughing. The fun and laughter made Mandy forget for a moment that she didn't live in their comfortable old apartment where she fit in. Even Caroline seemed to be her old self and not so bossy.

After fussing over Mittens, they all went to the vacant lot to play kickball until it grew too dark to see the ball. Kickball in the vacant lot with the Mikimoto children was much different than kickball in phys-ed class at Queen Anne School. Even Susan and Ben joined in. Baiko and Dayu were especially careful to kick the ball gently to the little ones.

Later, they went back in, laughing and hot and dusty and sweaty. Mrs. Mikimoto let them take their pie and glasses of milk into the boys' bedroom, where they turned on the radio and listened to *Inner Sanctum* and *The Shadow*. The grown-ups were listening to *The Hit Parade*, which was pretty boring.

Mandy had to move over a stack of comic books to make room to sit on the floor. The Mikimoto boys and John used to have contests to see who could collect the most Captain Marvel comics. The Mikimotos usually won. They had twice the allowance money as John.

The radio shows were spooky, and the boys wanted to turn out the lights and listen in the dark. And they did—until Susan started crying. Hideko quickly took Susan onto her lap, wiping away her tears and telling her everything was all right. Mandy thought that Ben looked just as scared, but he didn't cry.

After that, they left the lights on, but they still had a good time. And because it was such a special night, they were each allowed to have two pieces of pie. Susan couldn't eat all hers, so the boys finished it for her.

As they drove through brightly lit downtown Seattle back to Queen Anne Hill, Susan fell sound asleep, leaning heavily against Mandy's side. How Mandy wished the evening could have lasted forever.

When they stopped at the house, Dad came around to the backseat and gently lifted Susan up in his arms to carry her inside. As he did, she roused enough to ask in a sleepy voice,

"Daddy, what's an alien?" making all the rest of them laugh. Ben, however, was still wide-awake.

Later, Mandy lay awake, thinking about the fun she'd had that evening. She heard Lora coming in from her date, and she could hear through the walls Lora and Caroline's excited voices chattering together. Mandy bet Lora was telling Caroline all about her date, the places where she and Mark had gone, and the romantic things they'd done together.

She heard Lora turn on the phonograph and put on the Glen Miller recording of "Somewhere Over the Rainbow." Lora had lots of phonograph records, and lucky Caroline got to share them now that they were in the same bedroom.

When they'd lived at the Fairfax, Mandy and Susan slept in the upper bunks of the two bunk beds, and the older girls were below. Mandy would lay there pretending to be asleep, yet listening to the older girls' conversations. Now she was stuck off with the baby as though she, too, were a baby in the family. And they didn't have a phonograph player in their room.

Why couldn't Caroline have shared a room with Susan and let Mandy be with Lora? No one had even asked her opinion in the matter. Perhaps her opinions didn't even count.

Thick, foggy mist hung in the air as they left for church the next morning. Mark had come by early to pick up Lora. They sang in the choir, and extra rehearsals were held before Sunday school started. Lora came home so late and rose so early that Mandy wondered how her sister could go on so little sleep.

The big, stone church with its heavy bell tower stood at the edge of the downtown business district. Dad had promised them when they moved that they would continue attending their old church, for which Mandy was thankful. A few of the girls she'd gone to school with at Bailey Gatzert were in her Sunday school class. Everything had been fine during the summer. But now that school had started, her friends Sarah Marie and Liza were talking about activities at school, and none of it concerned Mandy.

When they asked about Queen Anne School, all she could say was, "It's okay." Which, of course, it was not. Not even close.

Mandy loved Pastor Martin. He was young and had a pretty wife and two little sons. His sermons were colorful and easy to understand. She hardly ever fidgeted when he preached. Which is more than she could say for Ben and John. They were always getting into trouble. Mama said John was a bad influence on Ben. Mandy agreed.

"John, you should be setting a good example," Mama would say in her exasperated tone.

"I'm trying," John would answer in a feeble attempt to defend himself.

"You're not trying hard enough," Mama would reply.

It was a conversation that everyone in the family knew by heart.

This morning, Pastor Martin was preaching from the book of 2 Samuel, using the story of Jonathan's crippled son who had the long name of Mephibosheth. King David had made an oath to show kindness to the family of his friend Jonathan, Pastor explained. After Jonathan had died and David became king, he remembered his promise and began to search the land for members of Jonathan's family.

Mandy turned to the passages in her small, white Bible. She followed along, listening to Pastor tell how David looked for Mephibosheth. When he found the man, he brought him into the king's house. But Mephibosheth was crippled in his feet.

"Poor Mephibosheth," Pastor said. "He was embarrassed and ashamed. He bowed down and said, 'What is thy servant, that thou should look upon such a dead dog as I am?'" Pastor Martin smiled. "What a surprise was in store for this man who was unable to walk normally. He was told that he would eat bread at the king's table every day."

Mandy thought about Helga being lame in her feet and the strange way she walked. She was sort of like Mephibosheth, although Mandy couldn't imagine brash Helga bowing down and saying she was like a dead dog.

"King David," Pastor continued, "sent for one of Saul's servants and commanded him and his sons and servants to till the land and bring the fruit of it to Mephibosheth." Closing his Bible, Pastor looked over the congregation and said, "God is faithful to His promises, even more so than King David. He doesn't care if we are lame or crippled. He loves us and wants us all to come and eat at His table."

As they stood to sing "Come and dine, the master calleth, come and dine," Mandy wondered if Helga knew that God loved her in spite of her crippled feet.

CHAPTER 5

Lora's Surprise

At school on Monday morning, Mandy met Miss LaFayette in the hallway. The librarian was dressed in a pale yellow dress with a knife-pleated skirt and softly bloused bodice. Her short, curly hair was fluffed perfectly around her small face, and her red lipstick was flawless.

"Good morning, Mandy," she said. As Mandy drew near, she caught a whiff of Evening in Paris cologne. Lora used that, too.

Mandy was surprised that the librarian had remembered her name. She mumbled her greeting and started to pass by, but Miss LaFayette stopped, so Mandy stopped as well.

"Did you finish your two books over the weekend?"

Mandy nodded, hoping no one was listening. She'd finished the books all right, but Caroline had called her a lazybones and accused her of reading as an excuse to get out of work.

"Tell you what," Miss LaFayette said. "Since you're such a book lover, if you get here a little bit early in the morning, come down to the library and I'll let you switch your two books for two more."

Mandy felt her heart skip a beat. "Honest? Could I do that?" She was wondering if she could force herself to get up earlier in the morning.

"You may do that," Miss LaFayette answered, her brown eyes smiling.

"Thank you very much," Mandy breathed, then hurried to put her books away.

Later, as the students filed into the classroom, one of the girls in the Golden Ring was mimicking Helga's strange way of walking. Everyone else laughed. Mrs. Crowley's back was turned, and she didn't seem to know anything was happening.

"Dummies." Helga dropped heavily into her seat, making her desk shake—and the one in front of her as well. "Bunch of dummies is all you are," she said in a grating whisper. Her words made them laugh all the more. Elizabeth and Jane hooked little fingers across the aisle.

Mandy realized they wanted Helga to say something. And she always did.

All the girls had purchased their gym suits, and showers after phys-ed class were required. Most of them turned on the water in the stalls, then jumped in quickly and back out just as quickly. Not Helga. She was the only one who stood inside the curtained stall for any length of time and actually used the soap.

One day after gym class was over, the hot, sweaty girls crowded into the locker room laughing and talking. When they'd done their usual spritz in and out of the showers, Mandy heard Jane Stevens say, "Hey, Elizabeth. Look here." Mandy turned to see that she was pointing to Helga's clothes lying in a rumpled pile along with the unsightly built-up shoes.

"Well, well," Elizabeth said, running her hairbrush through her long, silky hair. "What do you know? Dirty laundry."

The other girls giggled. Helga's dresses were plain and

unattractive, and her one red cardigan sweater, which she wore nearly every day, was frayed along the cuffs of the sleeves.

"What do we do with dirty laundry?" Elizabeth asked, laying her brush down on the edge of the sink.

"Why, we wash them, of course." This bit of wisdom came from Renee Ford. Mandy thought Renee looked much too innocent to be part of the Ring, but who could tell? Renee picked up the clothes with one hand, while holding her nose with the other. "Shall I?"

"Dirty laundry needs washing," Jane said with a smirk. "We're doing her a favor."

Renee dumped the clothes into a shower stall, and Jane tossed the shoes and stockings in after them.

Mandy quickly pulled on her skirt and blouse, acting as though she heard nothing. But inside she wanted to scream at them to stop. Her shoes and stockings were on in a flash, and she was going out the door of the locker room when she heard Helga hollering because her clothes were nowhere to be found.

How Mandy wished she could do something. But what? Her stomach was churning as she hurried back to class. Later, when class began, Helga was missing. Mandy learned later that the girls told Miss Bowen that Helga took a shower with her clothes on.

Would Miss Bowen have believed such a story? Maybe so. After all, everyone said Helga was not right in her head. Elizabeth and Jane said she was madder than a March hare. Mandy wasn't so sure about that. Just because her feet were crippled didn't mean her brain was.

Poor Helga was driven home by Miss Bowen and didn't come back to school that day.

Mandy had no trouble getting up the next morning. She was awake and dressed before Mr. Buckley, the milkman, pulled up to the house to deliver their daily milk and cream. When it was time to leave for school, John and the twins weren't at the front door waiting for her. She was there first.

When John asked why she was ready so early, she told him about Miss LaFayette's offer to let her come to the library before school.

"I like Miss LaFayette," Susan said as she skipped along beside them.

"Me, too," Ben echoed. "She's nice. She comes to our room and reads us a story. I sit on the blue circle at story time."

"I sit on the yellow circle. Yellow's my mostest favorite color. Sunshine is yellow."

As the twins walked ahead of them, John said, "You must've made an impression on the librarian. What did you do?"

Mandy smiled. "Actually, it's because I wasn't listening. I didn't hear her say we could only check out two books, and I had five. Had to put three of them back."

John laughed. "I guess only a librarian could appreciate that."

As they talked about school, Mandy considered telling him about the incident with Helga in gym class. How the girls had soaked Helga's clothes. But before she had a chance to decide, two boys from down the street called to him.

"See you later," John said and sprinted off. Mandy wished someone were calling to her to hurry and join them.

Before going downstairs to the library, Mandy glanced

about to see if anyone was watching. But it was early and the halls were nearly empty, so she felt safe.

Miss LaFayette smiled when Mandy came in. "Good morning, Mandy," she said, peering over a low bookshelf. "How's my fourth-grade avid reader?"

"Fine, thank you." Mandy felt warm inside. "Shall I lay these here?" She put her two books on the librarian's desk.

"Yes, please. I'll check them in later. Come here. I want to show you something."

Mandy followed her into a small room behind the check-out desk. Waving to a counter, Miss LaFayette said, "Here are the books that have just come in. They're ready to be put on the shelves, and I thought you'd like to see them first."

"Goodness gracious." Mandy breathed a deep sigh. "Do you really mean it?"

"Why, of course I mean it. Come take a look."

Mandy ran her fingers over the bright, shiny dustcovers. They were beautiful. So fresh and new. Out of the stack, she chose one novel and one biography.

"I'll take these." She suddenly felt very shy.

"Good choices. Come, let's check them out for you."

After the returned books were checked in and the new ones checked out, Mandy thanked Miss LaFayette. But the thank-you seemed paltry. She wished she could explain to this pretty lady just how much her kindness meant.

Mandy hurriedly took her things to the classroom, then went outside since no one was allowed to loiter in the halls before the bell rang. That afternoon, she'd be able to take one of her new books outside and read during recess.

Later, when they were all seated in Mrs. Crowley's classroom, Mandy heard someone say, "Hey, Einstein!"

At first Mandy ignored the voice, but the boy next to her tapped her shoulder. "Hey, brain," he said. "Elizabeth wants you."

She looked around, and Elizabeth pointed to Mandy's desk, where the brand-new library books lay in plain sight. Mandy cringed. She should have put them inside the desk so no one could see them.

"Where'd you get the new books, Mandy Einstein?" Elizabeth whispered. "Do you get special favors at the library?"

"She must be Miss LaFayette's pet," Jane said.

Mandy turned around to face the front and tried to ignore the chorus as they whispered, "LaFayette's little pet! La-Fayette's little pet!" over and over again.

That day in the locker room, Mandy was the target.

"Does anyone else in school get nice, new library books?" Elizabeth taunted as they were changing into their gym suits.

"Only the brain, Mandy Einstein," Renee chimed in.

Mandy said nothing, but her face felt hot and her stomach rolled so that she thought she was going to be sick. Later she wondered how she even made it through phys-ed class.

That afternoon, she took a book outside with her and sat far from the others under one of the few shade trees on the school grounds. She opened the first in the Elsie Dinsmoor series. Miss LaFayette had encouraged her to begin the series. "I've ordered the entire set," she had said. "They should be arriving next week."

Mandy didn't even notice that the Golden Ring had slipped up behind her, but when she looked up from her book, there they were. All four of them. She noticed their saddle oxfords were getting a little scuffed after a couple weeks of school. Especially Lily Madison's.

"I think that brand-spanking-new library book should have been mine," Elizabeth said in her lilting voice. "Don't you, girls?"

"I don't see why not," Jane agreed.

Mandy's heart pounded. Why couldn't they just leave her alone? She'd never bothered them.

"But then," Elizabeth went on, "I'm not a little pet." She shook her head and curled up her pretty lip in a mock pout. "I'm not as good as the brain here."

"But you can have the book if you want it, Elizabeth." Jane took a step closer.

Mandy tightened her grip on the book, but it was too late. Before she could think to wrap her arms around it, the book was snatched from her hands.

"Hey!" she said, springing up to her feet. "Give that back!"

"What do you know?" Renee squealed. "She really talks."

The four girls laughed and danced around, passing the book one to another while Mandy watched helplessly. Suddenly the bell clanged. Renee, who was holding the book, said, "My, oh my, time to go." With that, she deliberately dropped the lovely new book into the dirt, tearing the cover and bending the pages.

As the Golden Ring marched smugly away, they were hooking little fingers and laughing. Mandy rescued the book from the dirt and tried her best to wipe the pages clean with the skirt of her dress. Whatever would she tell Miss LaFayette?

Now she knew how Helga felt when she went home in wet clothes. She guessed having the school librarian for a friend wasn't such a good thing after all.

On Friday night, Mark came to supper at the McMichael house. Having worked on the docks for several years, Mark had rippling muscles and a broad chest. He was a happy guy with a broad smile and a shock of brown hair that fell across his forehead.

The two lovebirds pushed their chairs close to one another at the table. Every once in a while, Mark would reach over and touch Lora's hand. Mandy thought that would be terribly embarrassing, but it didn't seem to bother Lora one bit.

Seeing them so happy made Mandy feel sad inside. She wanted to be happy for them, but she felt too miserable. That morning she'd intentionally turned around the *i* and the *e* in the spelling word *receive*. She was determined never to get a perfect spelling score again. It was easier and simpler to miss one or two words each week on purpose. And that's exactly what she planned to do.

She wasn't sure how far she'd take her plan, but she could easily write shorter paragraphs in language class and mix up the state capitals in geography. There had to be a way to make the Golden Ring stop making fun of her. The plan to stop doing her best seemed to be the only way.

"But our army is pathetic," Mark was saying to Dad as they ate Mama's delicious pot roast.

Mandy suddenly became aware of the voices swirling around her. They were talking about war again.

Dad nodded grimly. "Pathetic is right. And that doesn't even take into consideration our lack of a fully equipped navy."

"Or the lack of air power," Peter put in.

Mandy cringed at their words. She hated when the conversation turned to war—as it always seemed to do.

"The totalitarian countries have more than fifteen hundred aircraft," Dad said, waving his fork in the air. "The United States may have about eighty. That's way out of balance."

Not wanting to be left out, John added, "Our teacher, Mr. Cutts, says that Britain has always controlled the seas and will keep on doing so without our help."

Dad shook his head. "But, Son, there's more to this than ruling the seas. This war will be won by the nation who rules in the air."

Mandy's father knew exactly what he was talking about. He helped design the airplanes that were being turned out at the Boeing plant. Those fighters and bombers were being shipped to Britain to help defend against the threat of attack from Nazi Germany.

Later, the family retired to the living room, where they listened to Fulton Lewis Jr., the radio news commentator from Washington, D.C. That meant even more talk about war and serious things.

Mandy went to her room to read a library book.

The next evening, as the family was in the living room after supper, they heard Mark's Ford drive up.

Mother looked up from her knitting. "What are the kids doing coming home at this hour?"

They all knew that, on Saturday night, the couple never arrived home until around eleven. Even then they would sit out in the Ford talking.

Soon Mark and Lora were standing side by side in the living room doorway, holding hands and looking rather sheepish.

"Mother, Daddy, everyone. . ." Lora stretched out her left hand. "Mark and I are engaged." But before anyone could react, she added, "And Mark has enlisted in the navy."

Mandy felt as though she'd been hit in the face with a bucket of ice water.

CHAPTER 6

The Lie

Mandy watched as her mother's face turned pale. Everyone froze, and the room was dead still for an endless moment.

The twins were sprawled on their stomachs, scribbling in their new coloring books. Suddenly, Susan leaped to her feet. "You're gonna be a bride, Lora? A real bride with flowers and a veil and everything?" She ran to hug her sister, breaking the awkwardness of the moment.

Lora gave a nervous laugh. "I don't know about all that, Susan. We've decided to wait to get married."

Mama sighed then. She and Dad were on their feet hugging Lora, shaking hands with Mark, and giving their congratulations.

"You're sure you know what you're doing, son?" Dad asked.

"Oh, yes, sir," Mark answered. "Lora and I've talked this over. I want to get into the service now before it all breaks loose."

Dad nodded. Mandy thought her father's eyes looked wet, and he was biting his lip.

Lora looked past her parents and said, "Well, what about the rest of you? Has everyone turned into zombies?"

Mandy didn't feel like congratulating them at all. Why did they want to get engaged if Mark was going to be leaving? It all seemed so senseless. And so scary. Especially when Mark said, "before it all breaks loose," as if he had no doubt that war was coming. She followed John and Caroline in giving hugs and her best wishes, but her heart wasn't in it.

Since Peter was still at work, Lora and Mark decided to run over to the Tydol station and tell him their news.

"They have more surprises than *Mystery Theater,*" John said after they were gone. He went back to his stack of comic books and started reading again.

They all tried to go back to what they were doing. Dad's newspaper was open again, but Mandy could bet he wasn't reading it.

"Mark's so young to be going away." Mama's voice was wistful. The knitting lay untouched on the lamp table beside her.

Dad put down his paper. "I know, Nora. But if war does come, boys younger than Mark will be called."

"I know, Paul. I remember," she said softly.

Of all things, why does Mark have to join the navy? Mandy wondered. Especially now, when German U-boats were shooting torpedoes at everything afloat. She didn't even want to think about it.

Late that night as she lay in bed trying to sleep, she could hear Caroline and Lora talking in low voices in their room. The phonograph was playing the yearning strains of "Red Sails in the Sunset." Mandy wondered if Lora was happy or sad. How could her sister bear to let Mark go away?

Mandy didn't return the soiled library book on library day because she didn't want the Golden Ring to see her. Instead, she waited until the next week, when she could go into the library early. The book didn't look all that bad, but there was a tear on the dust jacket.

She tried and tried to think of a way to tell Miss LaFayette what had happened to the book, but nothing seemed right. Being a tattletale was out of the question. She considered returning it and saying nothing, but that seemed terribly ungrateful after the librarian had been so kind to her.

Walking into the library, Mandy lay the book on the desk in front of Miss LaFayette. "Miss LaFayette," she heard herself saying, "do you have any little sisters or brothers?"

Miss LaFayette looked at the book, then looked up at Mandy, her doe eyes soft and kind. She nodded. "A younger brother."

Mandy pointed to the book. "Well, I have a little sister and a brother."

"The twins? Susan and Benjamin?"

"That's them," Mandy said, feeling her chest go tight.

Miss LaFayette smiled. "It happens, Mandy. I know you would never intentionally damage a brand-new book."

"No, ma'am," she answered honestly, "I never would."

Miss LaFayette gave her permission to check out another book. As she walked out of the library, Mandy told herself that she never actually said the twins did anything. So it wasn't really a lie. Then why did she feel so dirty inside?

Steam rose up in miniature clouds as Mandy smoothed the iron over one of John's starched shirts. The steam created a warm mixture of clean-outdoor and laundry-soap smells. There was so much starch in the shirt, she practically had to peel it off the ironing board to move it around.

Supper was over, and Mama had set up the iron and ironing board in the kitchen for her. *Fibber McGee and Molly,* one of Mandy's favorite programs, had just come on the radio. Every time Fibber opened a closet door, Mandy heard a frightful crashing noise as all the stored junk came tumbling out. She giggled every time it happened.

Caroline told her they used sound effects to make that kind of racket. Mandy supposed that was true. Nothing was real on the radio or at the movies. Except for the newscasts and newsreels. They were real. And they were scary.

"You're supposed to iron the yoke first." Caroline's voice intruded into her thoughts. "I thought you knew how to iron."

"I do know how to iron." Mandy held up the shirt and studied it. It wasn't as good a job as Mama would have done, but it looked good to her.

"Here." Caroline came around to the other side of the ironing board. "Let me show you."

Mandy stepped out of the way. She hated it when Caroline started acting like she was all grown up. Besides, Mandy was missing the best part of *Fibber McGee and Molly*. At supper, Caroline had accused her of setting the table the wrong way. What was next?

Caroline took the shirt from her. "Like this," she said as though she were showing Susan how to tie her shoes. "Fold the crease across the yoke and iron the yoke first, then the collar, then the sleeves, then the rest of the shirt, in that order. When you do it right, it won't look like a little kid ironed it."

Mandy took the shirt back from her sister, put it on the

hanger, and hung it on the rod with the rest of the dresses, shirts, skirts, and blouses. She looked at the clothes still in the laundry basket, every piece dampened and rolled up tightly to retain the dampness. At the bottom was one of Lora's full skirts. Yards of material to iron. She reached down, picked it up, and held it out to Caroline. "Here," she said. "Show me how to iron this skirt."

Caroline pressed her lips together and squinted up her eyes. "No need to get smart. I was just trying to help."

Mandy said no more, but she didn't see how being bossy could help anyone. She reached over and turned the radio up a little. As long as she listened to the radio programs or read a good book, she could ignore all the unpleasant thoughts chasing around in her head.

Just then, Lora came into the kitchen. "Ready for me to start on my half of the ironing?"

Mandy smiled. "I was ready before I started on this." She set the iron on its heel and waved at the full skirt draped over the ironing board.

"I'm surprised you didn't leave it for me." Lora put her arm around Mandy and gave her a squeeze. "You're a good worker, Mandy." She leaned over to plant a soft kiss on Mandy's cheek.

Mandy wanted to tell Lora that Caroline had accused her of being a lazybones, but she didn't think Lora needed to know anyone else's troubles. After all, she had enough on her mind with Mark leaving in two days.

"I'll finish the skirt if you'd like," Lora offered.

"Thanks." Mandy stood a moment, savoring the sweetness of Lora's presence. Surely Lora was dreading Mark's leaving, but her face didn't show it. "Guess I'll go do my homework," Mandy said.

"You do that. We want to see another string of A-pluses just like last year."

Mandy watched a moment as Lora deftly ran the iron over the skirt, smoothing out all the wrinkles. She wanted to tell her sister that this year was nothing like last year. Her family shouldn't look for the A-pluses from her. She wanted to tell Lora all about the wretched girls in the Golden Ring and about her lie to Miss LaFayette about the torn book. And about the plight of poor Helga. But she didn't. She turned and went up to her room.

They were all at the train station to see Mark off. All but Dad, who couldn't get off work. Mark was headed for San Diego for his basic training, then off to who knew where. His parents and sister were at the station already, and his mother couldn't stop crying. Lora clung to him. When the conductor called the final "All aboard," Mark almost had to tear himself away from her.

Steam hissed out in a cloud from beneath the wheels as the train began to move. At first the train moved slowly, then the pistons pumped louder as it picked up speed. The whistle sounded a long, loud blast that hurt Mandy's ears. Mark opened the window and hung halfway out, waving and waving. They all waved back until the entire train was gone and an awful silence filled the air.

Back home, Lora went up to her room and shut the door. Not even Caroline could go in. Mother said they were to leave Lora alone. "She'll come out when she's ready," Mama said.

Mandy knew that feeling. She wished she, too, could shut herself in her room and never come out again.

CHAPTER 7
Back to the Fairfax

October was soggy with rain and heavy with dreary skies. Mandy thought if she had to wear her red boots to school one more day, she'd just die. She hated wearing boots. And she hated staying inside at recess. Staying in at recess meant she couldn't escape the snooty Golden Ring, who seemed to gather power as the school year progressed.

Mama tried to talk her into eating a hot lunch in the lunchroom, but Mandy insisted she wanted to walk the twins home. In truth, she wanted to stay away from Queen Anne School just as much as she possibly could.

If the wretched weather wasn't enough, the first report cards were handed out. The sight of Bs and B-minuses on her card nearly made her sick. Mama's reaction was even worse. An awful look of disappointment came over her mother's face as she gazed at the card.

"Mandy, what happened to your As?" she asked.

"John got Bs on his card," she said in defense. "Why aren't you upset with him?"

Mama leveled a look at Mandy that made her want to melt away. "John's Bs are an improvement from the Cs he'd been making last year."

Mandy studied her shoe tops as she struggled with the shame and confusion. In order to avoid trouble in class, she had to disappoint her mother. Which was worse? She wasn't really sure.

"Fourth grade is lots harder than third," she said. But that wasn't true. None of it was really hard for her.

"I expect to see you spending more time on homework this next six weeks," Mama ordered.

All Mandy could do was nod her agreement.

A welcome break in the wet weather came the first week of November. Mandy was thankful to be out on the playground again for recess, away from the other kids. She huddled with her coat around her, reading another book in the Elsie Dinsmoor series. Even though the sun was out, the air was chilly. Midway through recess, she was distracted by shouts coming from another part of the playground. It was Helga again, only this time the boys were tormenting her.

She could hear them saying something about a circus. Putting her finger in her place in the book, she looked over at the commotion. They were playing circus, it seemed, and they'd set up a long two-by-four to serve as the tightrope.

"And here we have my pet bear," one of the boys shouted. Someone had looped a long piece of twine around Helga's neck. "Come on, *bruin*," the boy said. "Show the folks how you can walk the high wire."

Helga stepped up on the two-by-four, but her awkward, clumsy feet simply could not maneuver that board. As she slipped off again and again, the crowd of boys roared with laughter. Why was she allowing them to do that? Why wasn't she yelling at them?

"Roly, poly, big brown bear," they chanted through their laughter. "Roly, poly, big brown bear."

Mandy closed her eyes to shut out the ugly scene. Where were the teachers? They should stop this cruelty. And why didn't Helga's parents come to the school and stand up for her?

When Mandy opened her eyes again, she saw that John was right in the midst of all the rowdies. And he was laughing! When school let out that afternoon, she was determined to ask him about it. She couldn't believe he would do such a cruel thing.

John looked ashamed when she brought it up later, but he said, "I was only watching them. I sure didn't put that twine around her neck. And the game wasn't my idea."

He glanced over at her as they walked along. "Tell me, do you think I could have stopped them?"

She shook her head. Of course she didn't think that. If he could have stopped the game of circus, then she could have stopped the girls from putting Helga's clothes in the shower that day. She wanted to tell him that he should have walked away. But what good would that have done? It was so confusing. She didn't know what the answers were for poor Helga.

"Helga isn't what really bothers me, anyway," John was saying.

At first she wasn't really listening. Then it hit her that John was trying to tell her something. Something important. "Something else is bothering you?" she asked.

John paused a minute. "The guys I'm friends with, they say bad things about the Japanese. Alex Brown said the other day that he hates all Japs. He said his father calls them the Yellow

Peril and that we shouldn't trust any of them."

She waited for him to go on. When he didn't, she said, "A lot of people are saying those things these days." During the times they'd stayed indoors for recess, Mandy heard Elizabeth Barrington say that her father was a member of the America First Committee. He believed that all foreigners were a threat to the nation.

"Whenever I hear them talk like that and I don't tell them I disagree, I feel I've let Baiko and Dayu down." His pace slowed a little more. "It's an awful feeling."

Mandy was surprised that John was also struggling with problems. "I know what," she said. "Let's ask Mama if we can take the bus to Yesler Way on Saturday. Maybe we can spend time with Baiko and Dayu. That'd be fun, wouldn't it?"

John's face brightened a little. "That would be fun. We'll have to get our work done early, though, or Mama won't let us go."

"We can do it," she assured him. Having John tell her about his dilemma made her feel a little better about her own problems.

After Mama gave permission for them to go to the Fairfax on Saturday, the twins begged to go along. But Mama said a flat no. Mandy was glad. It would be just her and John.

Saturday was overcast, but the rain seemed to be holding off. They boarded the new "trackless trolley," the electric buses that needed no tracks. Unlike the old trolleys, the buses were connected to overhead wires by a long rod. The trackless trolleys were great because they could go places the old trolleys never could.

John had phoned the evening before to be sure Baiko and Dayu could spend the day with them. The Mikimoto boys had to finish their work quickly as well. And they had far more chores at the hotel than John and Mandy did at home. There was always sweeping and cleaning to do.

Mr. Mikimoto was busy at the hotel desk, and Mrs. Mikimoto was changing linens, so there was no one around to tell them to sit down in the kitchen and slowly sip a cup of tea from a handleless cup. Hideko and the boys met them at the door. Gentle Hideko invited them to come and see how Mittens was growing.

"She follows Hideko everywhere," Dayu said. "Father says Hideko and Mittens are closer than the little McMichael twins."

John laughed. "That's mighty close."

Mandy agreed. She couldn't imagine Susan and Ben not being together.

Hideko showed them how Mittens would curl around her neck like a little gray and white collar. "She rides there as I go about my work." Hideko reached up to stroke the soft fur. "She likes to be with me."

Mandy wished she could have a kitten of her own. But a kitten at the McMichael household would belong to everyone and not just to her.

"Let's go to the vacant lot," John said. "That's what we came for."

They quickly pulled on their jackets and ran out the back door that led into the alley. As they made their way down the alley, they passed warehouses and small manufacturing plants, some of which had windowpanes broken out.

Mandy pointed to them and asked, "What happened there?"

"Angry Seattle citizens," Baiko told her.

"What does that mean?" John asked.

"Those are Japanese-owned businesses. Like Father was telling you the other day, some people think we're responsible for what the Japanese are doing in China. So they just get mad at all of us."

Mandy shook her head. "That's not right."

Dayu looked over at her, his dark eyes sad. "It's scary, too."

The vacant lot was filled with some of the old friends they used to play with in the neighborhood. A game of kickball was already going, and the four easily joined in. After they tired of kickball, they chose sides and played Red Rover.

For Red Rover, they created two parallel lines by holding hands tightly. One team would cry out, "Red Rover, Red Rover, send Baiko right over." At that, Baiko would run as fast as he could into the line, trying to break it at its weakest point. If he broke through, he went back to his own side. If he was unable to break through, he had to join the opposite side. It hurt awful when someone hit your wrist hard, but everyone was a good sport. When the game was over, they all had sore wrists and cold noses.

It was time to go back to the hotel, grab a snack, then head to the movies together. It was just like old times.

"What's playing?" Mandy asked as they wolfed down peanut butter and jelly sandwiches.

"*The Wizard of Oz,*" Baiko mumbled around his sticky mouthful of sandwich.

"Have you seen it?" Dayu asked.

Mandy shook her head. "We haven't gone to the movies much since we moved. There's a theater in the neighborhood, but it's not right down the street like it is here."

"That's too bad." Baiko's tone made it sound like the most terrible catastrophe imaginable. And to him, it was. Both boys loved the movies.

After washing down their sandwiches with tumblers of iced Kool-Aid, they were out the door again. This time they ran out the front entrance and down the stairs.

"Do you have enough money for candy?" Baiko asked. He jingled change in his pocket. "Or shall we get popcorn at the theater?"

"Let's do both," John suggested. "Let's get Milk Duds at the drugstore and share them, then get two boxes of popcorn at the show and share them."

Baiko laughed. "What a great plan. Come on. I'll race you."

The four of them ran laughing and panting all the way up Jackson Street to the corner drugstore, where they purchased the Milk Duds. In the middle of the next block was the Palace Theater.

Mandy loved the first warm rush of the popcorn aroma that met her as she followed the boys inside the lobby. How she wished the Palace was in their new neighborhood. Here she first saw great shows like *The Little Colonel,* starring Shirley Temple, and some great Roy Rogers movies. The Palace was a very special place.

After paying their nickels for boxes of popcorn, they filed into the darkened theater and found seats near the front. The place was already packed with noisy kids.

"We'll have the popcorn first," Dayu said, "and save the Milk Duds 'til last."

As he spoke, the screen lit up and it was time for *Movietone News*. The newsreel told about the new Pan Am Airways plane that was making regular commercial flights to Europe. The plane was called the *Dixie Clipper*. People were flying over the Atlantic like they used to take a steamer, only the planes were much faster.

A sports clip showed the fall college football teams in heated games, with cheerleaders in their full skirts leading rousing cheers.

The scene changed then to Poland, where cameras scanned bombed-out shells of what were once buildings and stores and homes. The sudden takeover of Poland was called a *blitzkrieg*, which meant "lightning war." That's how fast the Nazi army could move. Mandy shivered at the gruesome sights.

The scene changed again and the narrator said, "The Japs show no signs of letting up their militaristic aggression in China." His tone made the word *Jap* sound as terrible as the word *Nazis*.

The scenes showed Japanese soldiers attacking the Chinese island of Hainan. "The strategy of the Japs," said the booming voice, "appears to be to leapfrog from China to the South China Sea. Will they then make a move to take over the entire Pacific?"

Mandy ached inside for Baiko, Dayu, and the other Japanese kids in the theater. How awful it must be for them to see their own countrymen fighting, killing, and dying.

The afternoon, which had started out being like old times and had been so much fun, was suddenly spoiled.

No matter how much she wanted it, life would never again be like old times.

CHAPTER 8

Mandy Speaks Up

Dad's long hours at the Boeing plant were hard on the entire family. When the twins acted up and got into mischief, Mama used to say, "We'll take care of this when your father gets home." But now the twins were asleep before Dad arrived home.

Every evening the twins seemed to get in some kind of scuffle. While they once were the same size, Ben was now getting long-legged and could get the upper hand quickly. That sent Susan crying and wailing to Mama. Mandy had never known them to be so cranky and out of sorts. Mama said it was because they needed their daddy.

Peter used to help with the little ones, but now he had all his homework to do when he came home from the Tydol station. And Lora was no help at all. As soon as supper was over, she disappeared to her room to write long letters to Mark and listen to "I'll Never Smile Again" and "Red Sails in the Sunset." Their family, it seemed to Mandy, was coming unraveled like the sleeves of Helga's red cardigan sweater.

Mandy was the one Mama often asked to play with the twins. "Will you keep them occupied until I get this done?" she'd ask.

Without fail, Mama would say this just as Mandy was ready to sit down and get lost in a good book. If she had to change clothes on the Shirley Temple doll one more time, she'd explode.

"Why can't Caroline watch the twins?" she'd say.

"Because," Caroline would answer in her know-it-all voice, "I'm helping Mama."

Mandy wanted to say, "I'll help Mama and you play with the twins," but she didn't want to make things any harder for poor Mama. She looked pretty tired as it was.

The wind off Elliott Bay had a bite to it as Mandy walked to school each morning. Brown construction-paper turkeys were taped up in the classroom windows. In their fourth-grade reader, they were reading stories about the Pilgrims and about Squanto, who had helped them through the first awful winter. Mandy thought about those brave people who made the journey across the ocean to a new world. Could those children have felt as lonely and empty as she did on this Thanksgiving?

When Lora first announced she planned to spend Thanksgiving Day with Mark's family, Mandy was crestfallen. How could her sister even think of leaving them on such a special day? But Mama came to the rescue.

"Our house is big enough," she said to Lora. "Invite them to come have Thanksgiving with us."

At that, Lora's eyes lit up—something that didn't happen much lately. That is, unless the postman brought her a letter from Mark.

What an odd Thanksgiving it was, to have guests who were practically strangers in the house. Mother warned the twins to behave themselves, and they did for a time. But before the pumpkin pie was served, Dad had to take them upstairs and give them a real talking-to. That helped some.

It seemed a shame that Dad was gone so much; then when he was home, he had to scold them. Later, Susan called Dad an old meanie. Only Mandy heard.

"Dad is not an old meanie," Mandy told her little sister. "And if you'd behave, he wouldn't have to scold you so much."

But Susan was too busy pouting to listen. She really could have won a Shirley Temple look-alike contest with that lower lip stuck out.

Mark's parents and sister were nice people. His sister, Betty, worked at the telephone company as a phone operator, and she and Lora were becoming good friends. Still, it just wasn't the same as being with the Mikimotos.

When the second report cards came out, Mandy took her turn at being scolded by Dad.

"I didn't tell your father the first time," Mama said to her. "I was giving you a chance to bring these grades up." She shook her head in dismay as she studied the card in her hand. "Now I'm afraid I have no choice. I'll have to discuss this matter with him."

So on Saturday morning, when she was usually listening to *Let's Pretend* on the radio, Mandy was in Mama and Dad's bedroom, receiving her scolding. She wanted to agree with Susan— Dad was an old meanie.

Why would they get upset with her for bringing home a card full of Bs? Well, there was one C in spelling. Perhaps she'd lost track of how many words she'd intentionally missed. She'd have to be more careful next time.

Neither parent asked her what the problem was. Or even if there was a problem. All they did was demand that she work harder and get her grades up.

Dad said, "Mandy, your mother and I know you can do better than this. It's important to do your best in everything you do. You understand that, don't you?"

She nodded, but she really didn't understand at all.

At school the next Monday, Mrs. Crowley announced that there would be tryouts for the annual Christmas pageant, which sent whispers rushing around the room like dry leaves in a December wind.

"You'll be Mary," Mandy heard someone saying to Elizabeth. "And the rest of us will be angels."

One of the boys added, "And Helga will be the donkey."

He said it so loud and there was so much laughter that old Mrs. Crowley actually heard the commotion. "Here, here," she said, tapping the desk with her pencil and peering at them over her small reading glasses. "We'll have no more outbursts. Noisy children will be sent to the principal's office. Do you hear?"

"We hear better than you do," Elizabeth whispered under her breath.

"Dummies," Helga said.

Stifled snickers spurted out in little bursts. But their hard-of-hearing teacher was oblivious.

Mandy wasn't about to try out for a part. She settled for singing carols with those who didn't receive special parts. As it turned out, a sixth-grade girl was chosen to be Mary. Secretly Mandy was glad. It was about time Elizabeth Barrington learned she couldn't have everything her own way. Elizabeth got the part of an angel, but not all her friends made it. Two members of the Golden Ring wound up as town folk standing around the inn in Bethlehem.

John, she learned after school that afternoon, had been selected as the innkeeper. Mandy could tell he was pleased as punch about it, too.

Risers were set up on the stage in the auditorium. A week before the pageant, they began practicing. Mrs. Sebastian, the music teacher, lined them up according to size and the parts they sang. When everyone had their positions, Mandy was on the end of the second row, with Helga directly behind her. It wasn't pleasant. The girl couldn't carry a tune in a bucket. Every note was off key. It was the worst singing Mandy had ever heard.

Amazingly, Dad was able to take off work for the performance. Mandy wondered if he made a special effort because John had such a special part. Or was it because the twins begged him to come? The kindergartners were going to sing "Away in a Manger" as a prelude to the pageant, and both Susan and Ben were giddy with excitement about being a part of the show, as they called it.

Mandy didn't get to see how well her younger siblings did with their parts. She was with the choir out in the hallway, waiting for their entrance. When the piano began playing "Silent Night," that was their cue to file in. Half of the group came in on one side of the auditorium, half on the other. Up the steps they went onto the stage.

Everything was going fine until they got to the risers.

Somehow Helga's built-up shoe got entangled with the risers or with her other shoe—Mandy was never quite sure which. She saw the big girl start to fall, then made the biggest mistake of her life. She reached out to help. As she did, she felt herself being dragged down slowly, slowly, with nothing to grab onto to catch herself or to stop the fall. She heard an awful *oof* as Helga landed on the boards. Mandy landed unceremoniously right beside her.

"Hey, Gottman," someone whispered, "I thought donkeys were supposed to be sure-footed."

"Tottery-doddery Gottman," whispered someone else.

Mrs. Sebastian came running over to see if everyone was all right. A sixth-grade girl whom Mandy didn't even know kindly reached down to give her a hand up. She mumbled her thanks, but her face was burning from embarrassment. With Mrs. Sebastian's help, Helga clumsily got back up on her feet. As she did, she glared at Mandy as though Mandy had been the cause of it all.

"It's all right," the music teacher said with a smile. "It could have happened to anyone. As they say on Broadway, 'On with the show.' "

Mandy didn't know how she made it through the rest of the evening. Her ankle ached, and her shin was scraped and raw. But the embarrassment from falling in front of the packed crowd was worse than anything else. Never had she been so humiliated.

Afterward, as they were driving home, Mama said that Mandy had handled herself very well. "I was proud of you." Then she added, "I feel so sorry for that lame girl. You'd think in this day and age she could have surgery to correct that problem."

But it was John and the twins who received all the attention. John had been a real hit as the innkeeper, and Dad bent over backward to fuss over the twins, telling them what a good job they'd done. Mandy saw how they basked in his praise.

She wished she'd never seen or heard of Helga Gottman.

After the pageant, there was yet one more week before Christmas vacation. Mandy could hardly wait. What a welcome break to be away from Queen Anne School from Christmas until after New Year's Day.

The fourth-grade room was festooned with loops and loops of red and green paper chains. Cardboard stars wrapped in tin foil dangled from the ceiling.

Christmas was supposed to be a time of peace and goodwill, but the Golden Ring didn't seem to know that. They continued to heap sarcasm and harassment upon poor Helga. Finally it happened. Mandy had had all she could stomach.

They'd just come into the locker rooms from a rough game of kickball where everyone in fourth grade seemed to make the ball hit Helga.

"Hey, tottery, doddery Gottman," Jane Stevens called out. "Step up here on the bench and show us how you took a flying leap at the Christmas pageant."

"Yeah," echoed Renee. "Show us. We want to see you do it again."

"And get Mandy Einstein to join her," Elizabeth said. "The two of them make a great team."

Mandy was sitting on the bench tying her shoes. Suddenly she stood up. "Oh, why don't you all just stop it? Don't you ever get tired of hurting people?"

You could have heard a pin drop. Every girl in the fourth grade was staring at her like she'd lost her mind. Then Elizabeth began to snicker. Another girl laughed out loud. Pretty soon everyone was laughing at her. Mandy sat back down and finished tying her shoes, but she felt like her face and ears were on fire.

Just then, clumsy Helga came limping by her on her way out the door. She leaned down and in her thick voice said, "Who asked for your help, little Miss Goody-Two-Shoes? I don't need you!"

Mandy stared at the girl as she made her step-roll way out the door of the locker room.

CHAPTER 9

In the Library

Everyone in the McMichael family was overjoyed when Dad announced they would be spending New Year's Eve with the Mikimotos.

"You mean it, Dad?" John said. When Dad assured him that he really did mean it, John exploded with a loud "Wa-hoo!" And Mama had to make him quiet down.

Both Dad and Mama voted that they were to spend their first Christmas in the new house right there at home. There was plenty of space in the living room for a big tree. The day they brought the tree home and set it up, Lora received a letter from Mark. Since she was in such good spirits, she pitched in and helped decorate. Even Peter was there to help.

After all the gifts were opened on Christmas morning, they telephoned the Mikimotos to wish them a Merry Christmas. Mandy was sad that even though they wanted the Mikimotos to come visit their house on Queen Anne Hill, it wasn't possible. They never discussed it, but they all knew Japanese people were safer and wiser to stay in their own neighborhood these days. It didn't make any sense, but that's just the way things were.

New Year's Eve came on Sunday, which was perfect. The Tydol station was closed, and Dad was off work. Although

Lora would much rather have been with Mark, he was hundreds of miles away. So they all piled into the DeSoto and drove to Yesler Way.

Susan was snuggled on Peter's lap, Ben was balanced on Caroline's lap, and Mandy had to awkwardly sit on Lora's lap, although she thought she was much too big to do so. Lucky John sat up front between Mama and Dad. No one suggested that he sit on anyone's lap.

In spite of the uncomfortable car ride, Mandy thought it was the most perfect New Year's ever. They played games, listened to radio programs, and ate yummy food—both Japanese and American. Games of Monopoly and Parcheesi went on for hours amid laughter and good-natured teasing.

Midway through the evening, the Mikimotos' preacher and his wife stopped by to give their regards. Mandy remembered the Reverend Timothy Smith as one of the regular visitors to the Fairfax when the McMichaels lived there. Pastor Smith, a portly man with graying hair and a kind smile, had once been a missionary to Japan. Both he and his wife spoke fluent Japanese. In fact, when the preacher and his wife spoke in Japanese to Mr. and Mrs. Mikimoto, their own children could barely understand what the adults were saying.

The extra guests squeezed into the small living area with the rest of them and accepted cups of tea and small cookies. After they'd eaten, Pastor Smith asked if he could pray for his parishioners. Mandy quickly learned that the pastor prayed much longer prayers than their own Pastor Martin.

By the time Pastor Smith and his wife left, it was nearing midnight. The twins fell asleep and were carted off to one of the bedrooms. Then the mood became more serious.

"It is not only a new year," Mr. Mikimoto was saying, "but a new decade as well."

"The past decade wasn't a very good one," Peter said, "with the Depression, the drought, and the terrible dust storms."

"But the 1930s brought us here to Seattle," Dad put in, "and gave me a great job."

Mama nodded. "There are always blessings if you just look for them."

Mandy wished that were really true. She tried to think of blessings at school, but she couldn't think of any. Well, there was one—Miss LaFayette. But only one!

"Mr. McMichael," said Mr. Mikimoto, "I have a request to make of you."

"I owe much to you, my friend," Dad replied. "Name your request."

"God forbid that there would ever be war between the country of Japan and our great United States. But should it come to pass, and I am. . ."

Mr. Mikimoto stopped a moment, and the room grew quiet. Mandy wondered what he thought might happen.

Troubled, he started again. "Should such a state of affairs come to pass and should something happen to me, might I ask you to watch over our children?"

"I'm sure such a thing would never happen," Dad assured him. "You may not be a citizen, but the entire community knows your reputation as an honest and upstanding person. If it will comfort your mind, however, I give you my word."

"Thank you," Mr. Mikimoto said, his voice quavering. "Thank you so very much." He lifted up his cup of tea. "To the

1940s. May they be good to all of us."

The grown-ups lifted their cups of tea, and the children lifted their glasses of Coca-Cola. "To the forties," they echoed and drank a toast.

"While I would like to toast to peace," Dad said, "it would seem there is no peace anywhere in the world tonight. So I pray that during this terrible time, people would come to know the Prince of Peace."

Mama touched Dad's arm. "I think that's a prayer, not a toast."

Dad blushed. "I suppose you're right, Nora. I'm not much at this toasting business."

"Then we shall pray," said Mr. Mikimoto. "Pray that no matter what happens, God will be our protector and our guide."

"Amen to that," said Lora.

They all knew her mind was on Mark.

Just as Dad closed his prayer, the melody of "Auld Lang Syne" came over the radio. Smiling, Mama joined in on the chorus, "For auld lang syne, my dear. . ."

Dad's baritone blended with her soprano, "For auld lang syne. . ."

Then they all joined in. "We'll take a cup o' kindness yet, For auld lang syne." Mama and Dad knew the words to all the verses, and their voices blended beautifully together. As the last strains faded away, they all shouted, "Happy New Year!"

It was officially 1940.

The morning Mandy returned to school following holiday break, she arrived early and hurried downstairs to the library.

Except for the books she'd received as Christmas gifts, she'd had no new books to read for over a week.

"Welcome back, Mandy." Miss LaFayette's voice was as cheery as ever. "I've been thinking about you over vacation time."

"About me?" Mandy placed her books on the desk.

"About you. Since you're such a book lover, how would you like to work here in the library with me?"

At first, Mandy thought she might be teasing. Growing up in a big family, Mandy was used to teasing. And Miss LaFayette's invitation seemed almost too good to be true.

"When would you want me to work?" she asked.

"It's winter now, and the weather will be messy outside—would you mind giving up two afternoon recesses a week?"

Now she knew Miss LaFayette was serious. Mandy would gladly give up every recess and phys-ed class to boot. "Oh yes," Mandy said, letting the excitement soak deep inside her. "I'd love to help."

How fun it would be to be among the stacks of books, helping to log them and put them away. But then another thought hit her. What would the Golden Ring say about this? It would give them just one more thing for them to torment her about.

"What is it, Mandy?" Miss LaFayette was studying her face. "Is something wrong? Perhaps it's not such a good idea. Perhaps I'm asking an awful lot."

Phooey on the Golden Ring. What did they know anyway? She'd taken all their rude remarks before. "Nothing's wrong, Miss LaFayette. Nothing at all. When do I start?"

The librarian smiled as she pulled the cards from the card file to check in Mandy's returned books. "As soon as I clear it with Mrs. Crowley and the principal."

By the next week, Mandy was slipping out of the classroom at the beginning of recess to go work in the library. Miss La-Fayette taught her how to put books on the shelves in proper order and how to file the cards correctly in the wooden card files. Together they decorated the bulletin board in the hallway outside the library. Just being among all the books would have been joy enough, but to work with Miss LaFayette was next to heaven.

The reactions from the Golden Ring came soon enough. "LaFayette's little pet," was whispered in the classroom. That wasn't too bad. But in the locker room one day, it took a different twist.

"Were you asked to work in the library?" Elizabeth asked someone. As usual, Mandy stayed as far away from the Ring as she could and kept her back turned as well.

"Why, no," came the reply. "Were you?"

"Me? Of course not. I'm not anyone's pet."

"Why do you think the new girl and the new librarian are so buddy-buddy?"

"I don't know."

Mandy's shoelace was in a knot. As her heart pounded, she fumbled to get it loose so she could get out of there.

"Maybe because they're both Jap lovers," came the unmistakable voice of Elizabeth Barrington. The statement brought gasps from the others.

"Mandy Einstein is a Jap lover?" Renee's shrill voice asked.

"She used to live with Japs." Elizabeth's voice was filled with disdain. "What do you think of that?"

Mandy's other shoe was on and tied, and she almost ran out

of the locker room. Her palms felt all sweaty, and her mouth felt like it was stuffed with cotton balls. The Golden Ring was shooting at her with both barrels. Was there no mercy?

Lora was practically flying around the house. She sang and whistled and laughed as she urged the rest of the family to help get the house spotless. Mark would be home for a week's leave before being shipped out.

When she first read his letter, which gave the details, Lora's face had turned pale. "The Philippines? Mark's being sent to the Philippine Islands." She stared at the letter in her hand.

"He had to be sent somewhere," Mama had said in her gentle voice. "You didn't think he'd be sitting in California for his tour of duty."

"No, of course not." Lora folded the letter then and put it away. "Well, he's going to be home for a few days. And we're going to make the best of it."

That's when the cleaning binge began. The only trouble was that everyone was supposed to be involved. Even Caroline balked. Mandy had seldom seen Lora and Caroline get into a fuss. But this was one time they did.

Caroline told her older sister to stop bossing her around. And Lora accused Caroline of not caring about this most important event in her life. It sounded rather childish to Mandy, who stared at her sisters in disbelief. Mama finally had to step in and calm them down.

"Lora, you're overwrought, my dear," Mama told her. "We all know this is a trying time for you, but you can't take it out on others."

"I was only asking for help!" Lora said, and with that she burst into tears and ran up to her room.

Caroline just shrugged her shoulders.

Mandy wished she could make Caroline understand that she was ten times more bossy than Lora ever thought about being. But Mandy didn't want to make matters worse.

Lora asked for some days off work when Mark came home. She said she didn't care if she got fired. She was going to spend every moment possible with her fiancé. Of course, she didn't get fired. In fact, her boss at the shipping firm told her he was proud of Mark for joining up. He gave her the entire week off.

Mama, Caroline, Mandy, and Lora were in the kitchen getting the special welcome-home supper prepared when they heard the Ford. Lora went flying out the back door. Mandy was sure her sister's feet never touched the steps. Mandy ran to the window just in time to see Mark jump from his car, grab Lora, and swing her round and round. When they stopped twirling around, he leaned down and kissed her—it seemed like forever. Mama said for her to get away from the window, but Caroline was staring, too, so Mandy didn't move.

When Mark came in the back door with Lora, Mandy couldn't believe he was the same person. He was dressed in his navy blue bell-bottom trousers and loose-fitting shirt, with a white sailor hat perched jauntily on his head. His hair was cut short, and he stood ramrod straight. Tall and proud. It took Mandy's breath away. He never looked that handsome when he was just a longshoreman on the docks. How would Lora ever be able to say good-bye to him a second time?

CHAPTER 10

Quiz Contest

Mandy was right. Saying good-bye to Mark a second time was devastating for Lora. She didn't talk as much as she used to. She didn't smile as much, either. Mandy thought her oldest sister shouldn't be sitting around listening to "I'll Never Smile Again" on the phonograph over and over again. But no one was asking Mandy's opinion.

After a couple weeks, Lora volunteered for the "Bundles for Britain" relief work, which kept her away from home more than ever. That meant she wasn't there to help with the bushel baskets of ironing anymore. Lora said it was important that she be involved in humanitarian work since she was engaged to a sailor on a warship.

Caroline said that ironing for the family was humanitarian, but Mama told her to hush. Mandy tended to agree with Caroline on that point. It seemed to Mandy that Lora should do her fair share whether she was helping send supplies to Britain or not.

One Saturday afternoon when much of the housework was finished, Mandy was headed to her room to finish a library book. As she passed the bedroom of her older sisters, Caroline called out, "Hey, Mandy. Come here a minute."

Mandy stopped in her tracks. "Are you talking to me?"

Caroline laughed. "Know any other Mandys that might happen to be in our upstairs today?"

Mandy laughed, too. "I guess not." She stepped inside. The older girls' room always smelled nice, like Evening in Paris and To a Wild Rose body powder. The phonograph was vibrating with a swing number played by Tommy Dorsey's orchestra. Both Lora and Caroline liked the sound of the swing bands. Mandy wondered if Caroline had permission to use it while Lora wasn't there.

Caroline was sitting at the dressing table brushing her hair in an upward sweep. "What do you think?" She turned around while holding the hair up off her neck. "Do I look older?"

"A little bit." Mandy sat down on the bed. Actually she didn't think the hairdo made her sister look any different at all.

"Mandy, do you think Mama would ever let me go on a date?"

Mandy was shocked. "A date?"

"Oh, not a real date like in a car. But maybe go with a boy to the drugstore after school for a malt?"

Mandy hadn't the slightest idea what Mama might say. Nor did she have the slightest idea why Caroline would be asking her, of all people. "I guess all you can do is ask," she offered lamely.

Caroline turned around to face the mirror. "You're probably right." She let the handful of hair drop and began brushing it again. "I know I'm not as pretty as some of the girls in school, but there's this boy. Randall is his name. Well, he started talking to me. Our lockers are next to each other." Caroline smiled as though they were sharing a good secret. "It's a swell way to get to know each other."

Mandy wasn't sure how to answer, but she tried to think of something so Caroline wouldn't stop talking to her. "That is a great way. We don't have lockers in grammar school."

"Well, you will in junior high. Sometimes having a locker is a pain in the neck. But when a nice boy has the one next to you, it can be a good thing."

Mandy was thinking that, with her luck, she'd have a locker next to Elizabeth Barrington.

"Anyway," Caroline went on, "he's asked me if I'd share a malt with him after school someday."

"Did he say which day?"

Caroline shook her head. "Just someday." She got up from the dressing table and did a few dance steps as she came across the room. "I'm learning to dance. One of the girls at school knows how to do the boomps-a-daisy. She's teaching me."

Mandy nodded, trying to look as though she were old enough to truly be sharing this conversation when she really wasn't. She'd never heard of such a thing as boomps-a-daisy.

Caroline sat down beside her on the bed and reached out to touch Mandy's shoulder-length hair. It was as though Caroline were looking at her, truly looking at her, for the very first time. "Are you going to wear your hair straight like this forever?"

Mandy shrugged. "I'm not as good as you are with hairdo ideas."

"Have you thought about cutting it? Then you can pin it up in pin curls and it would be fluffed around your face."

Mandy gave a little shiver. It sounded wonderful. "I don't even know how to make pin curls."

"Nothing to it." Caroline gave a wave of her hand. "You just take a strand like this." She lifted a strand of her own hair. "Then you wrap it around your first finger like this." She chuckled. "It's a little easier when it's wet and has some Dep on it. When it's all wound, you pull your finger out, hold the curl in place, and put in the bobby pins."

She demonstrated by opening a bobby pin with her teeth, then slipping it over the pin curl. Another bobby pin was put in to form an X on the curl and she was finished. "It's that simple."

Mandy had seen both Lora and Caroline with their hair up in pin curls, but neither of them had ever taken the time to show her how to do it.

"Do you think Mama would let me get my hair cut?"

Caroline jumped off the bed. "As you just told me, all you can do is ask."

Mama said yes to both girls. Caroline was allowed to stop at the drugstore with Randall, but only once a week and only for forty-five minutes. Caroline was delighted. And Mandy was delighted that she was going to get her long hair cut off. Now Mama couldn't look at her and say, "Mandy, why don't you go braid your hair?"

With her hair shorter and curlier, Mandy felt different somehow. She knew the girls at school wouldn't treat her any differently, but that didn't really matter. When she looked in the mirror, she liked what she saw. Even Peter complimented her on how it looked.

Her arms got tired sometimes when she was putting up her

pin curls each night. Especially the ones in the back. But she wouldn't complain. She figured it was part of growing older. Lucky Susan. Her hair was so curly she'd never need pin curls.

On a morning in mid-March, Mandy entered the front hall of the school and saw an entire set of encyclopedias sitting on a long table. Above the set of books hung a big sign that read, "WIN A SET OF ENCYCLOPEDIAS. QUIZ CONTEST, APRIL 19."

Mandy had no idea what a quiz contest was, but she soon found out. Mrs. Crowley handed out forms that explained the details. The contest was for fourth-, fifth-, and sixth-graders. Those entering the contest were to answer questions ranging from geography and history to grammar and arithmetic. The contest, it said, was to be held in the school auditorium. And the grand prize was the set of encyclopedias.

For a brief moment, Mandy considered filling out the form and entering the contest. How she would love to have that set of books on the shelves of the McMichael living room. But remembering the last attack from Elizabeth and her little group, she felt it wasn't really worth it. Who needed any more grief? She folded up the paper, stuffed it into her desk, and put it out of her mind.

Her birthday was right around the corner, and she was excited about finally turning ten. That was a much more pleasant thought than any old quiz contest.

A few days before the big day, Mama and Caroline asked her if she wanted to invite any of her friends over for a little party.

Mandy hesitated. She wasn't sure what to say. Mama and

Caroline glanced at one another. How could she tell them she didn't have even one friend at Queen Anne School? Mama had always preached to them that to have a friend you must be one. She sure didn't want to be accused of not being a good friend.

And Caroline was always telling her that she hid behind her books. "You need to stop reading so much and have a little fun," she'd say.

So when they asked about inviting friends, she shook her head. "Thanks for the offer, but I'd rather be with family."

"All right," Mama said. "It's your birthday."

Mama outdid herself by baking a high, light angel food cake with pink seven-minute frosting fluffed all over it. She topped it off with ten pink candles.

Several brightly wrapped gifts were on the sideboard in the dining room. Mandy could hardly wait for dinner to be over so she could open them. But first they had to light candles, and then everyone sang "Happy Birthday" to her.

"Should we wait until your father gets home before opening gifts?" Mama asked with a twinkle in her eye.

"No, no," the twins called out in unison as though the gifts were theirs. "We'll be asleep before Daddy gets home."

But Mandy knew Mama was teasing, and soon the twins knew it as well. The little ones were in charge of bringing the gifts to her. The first gift was a pair of brand-new roller skates. She'd been using old ones that had belonged to Lora and Caroline. Now she had a pair all her own.

The next gift was shaped like a shoebox. Sure enough, inside the wrapped box was a pair of black-and-white saddle oxfords.

Caroline smiled. "I told Mama to get them for you," she

said. "Everyone's wearing them this year."

As if Mandy didn't know. She lifted them up and inhaled the good smell of new shoe leather.

The last package, which was signed from all her brothers and sisters, was the best of all. Two pairs of dungarees. Blue denim dungarees just like the girls in the Golden Ring wore every Friday—with their pant legs rolled up just above the top of their socks. Mandy hugged the dungarees to herself and laughed right out loud. What a wonderful gift.

"Thank you, everybody. Thanks so much." And she went around hugging everyone. Even John, who said he was ready for a second piece of cake!

Mandy felt great wearing her dungarees and new saddle oxfords to school on Friday. And of course, Friday was library day, so it was a double-good day. When Miss LaFayette saw her, she raised her eyebrows and grinned. "You look great," Miss La-Fayette said softly so no one else could hear.

Mandy thanked her as though she were used to receiving such a compliment. Inside, she was turning cartwheels. As usual, she grabbed a couple books, headed to the reading area, and sat down at one of the tables where she could be alone. Later, she sensed that someone was nearby browsing the magazine racks where the *Jack & Jill* and *Wee Wisdom* magazines were kept.

Then she heard a voice say, "Mandy McMichael, for being an Einstein, you sure are dumb."

Mandy turned around and looked straight at Helga Gottman.

CHAPTER 11

Take Me Out to the Ball Game

Mandy was shocked. Helga hardly ever talked to her. And now that she had, she'd called her dumb. What was going on? Mandy turned back to her book and ignored the remark.

Once again came Helga's grating whisper. "You are so dumb." Mandy glanced up at the girl again. She was flipping through an old issue of *Jack & Jill*, acting as though nothing had happened. Mandy went back to her book.

"You're dumb to let all those snobs tell you how to act. I don't let them tell me how to act, and you're smarter than I am by a long shot." Mandy heard the magazine hit the shelf as Helga put it back. "You're so dumb to let those silly girls cheat you out of a set of encyclopedias." She stepped closer to where Mandy was sitting, the shuffle of her built-up shoe sounding on the wooden floor. "You're the only one in fourth grade who could really show 'em up," she said as she walked by. "Why don't you do it?"

Over the weekend, Mandy had a lot of time to ponder Helga's remark. It was true. She lay awake thinking about it. Why had she allowed those girls to force her into missing spelling words? And letting her schoolwork slide? And getting bad grades—all on purpose?

Just so they wouldn't make fun of her? They made fun of her

anyway. No matter what she did. For the first time, Mandy saw this was a losing battle. So why continue to battle? Helga never changed being who she was just to please the Golden Ring.

During her next worktime in the library, Mandy asked Miss LaFayette, "What would a person have to study to be able to compete well in the quiz contest?"

Miss LaFayette's eyes lit up. "Have you entered?"

"Not yet. I'm just thinking about it."

"I was hoping you would. It'd be a good experience for you. A student who reads as much as you do already has a broad knowledge in a number of areas." Miss LaFayette pulled out a pencil and said, "Tell you what. While you do the filing, I'll make a list of a few books that might help." Then she asked, "Do you have someone at home who would ask you questions?"

Mandy smiled. "I have a whole houseful."

"Oh, one more thing." Miss LaFayette reached over to the corner of her desk and handed her a form. "Be sure and enter!"

Every week, Mrs. Crowley gave a practice spelling test on Wednesday and the graded test on Friday morning. Anyone who made a perfect score on Wednesday didn't have to take the Friday test. Mandy made up her mind that from now until school was out, she was going to try to make a perfect score on every practice test. Just like that, she decided to stop failing on purpose. And it felt so good! Wait until Mama and Dad saw her next report card.

When she made a perfect score on the Wednesday test, the whispers started fast and furious. But this time it didn't really matter. Like Helga said, why should she let those girls tell her how to act? God gave her a brain, and she was going to use it.

At home, Mandy began to study like crazy, using the books that Miss LaFayette suggested. Mandy pestered Mama, John, and Caroline to ask her questions. When one got tired, she turned to the next. Mama seemed pretty happy that her daughter was serious about her studies again.

"I really want to win that set of encyclopedias," she told Caroline one evening. They were sitting on Caroline's bed, and Caroline was asking her questions out of a history book. Ever since their talk when Caroline had told her about Randall, Caroline had started talking to her more. She even told her details of what Randall was like and how much fun they had at the drugstore.

Caroline might have been lonely because Lora was gone so much. Mandy didn't care what the reason was; she was just glad Caroline was no longer treating her like a baby.

"You're going to be competing with kids two years older than you are," Caroline reminded her as she scanned the questions.

"I know," Mandy said. "I haven't forgotten. But I still want to win the encyclopedias."

Caroline laughed. "I guess it's good to have a goal."

Mandy had barely a month to prepare, and she was determined to make the most of every second.

With the arrival of spring came more bad news from Europe. Hitler had overrun Denmark and taken over Norway, and the German army did it with such speed and surprise that neither country could mount a defense.

Mandy watched her father's face grow serious as he listened to the radio news and discussed the war with Mama. He would shake his head in bewilderment and say, "I don't see how we can stay out of it much longer."

Dad was pleased when Neville Chamberlain was no longer prime minister of Britain. When Winston Churchill took his place, Dad said, "Now things will change for the better." Mandy sure hoped that was so.

Spring also brought with it complications in John's breathing problems. Sometimes Mandy could hear him coughing in the night. Hard, deep coughing. She wished she could do something to help. It must be awful to have such trouble breathing.

Mama was always telling him to be careful. Not to over-exert. Not to get overtired. And on and on. But he never listened. Mandy watched him at recess, and he played just as hard as all the other boys. But she'd never tell Mama.

Peter was also getting baseball fever. He kept saying he was going to get tickets to one of the Rainiers' home games. Mandy never dreamed that might include her, but one night at supper he said to her, "Hey, little sister, do you think you could take one Saturday afternoon off from your new study binge?"

"I don't know," she answered. "Why?"

Peter gave her a grin and winked. "I finally have tickets to the Rainiers' game."

"Hey," John spoke up. "You were gonna take me to that game, not her."

"Well, actually, John, I'm taking both of you."

Mandy thought surely she must be dreaming. She'd wake up in a minute and her brother would say he was only teasing. Could it be that Peter was actually taking her to a ball game?

"And that's not all," Peter added. "We're taking Baiko and Dayu as well."

John cheered. "Peter, you're the best brother ever in the whole world."

But just like a boy, instead of John giving Peter a hug, the two of them started wrestling right in the middle of the kitchen. Mama made them stop. "Before you break something," she said. But she was smiling when she said it.

To keep peace in the family, Mama planned to take the twins to the zoo at Woodland Park the same afternoon as the ball game. Caroline, it turned out, had a day-long baby-sitting job for a family up the street.

It rained all week, and Mandy began to wonder if the game would be rained out. As Saturday grew nearer, she found herself praying for good weather. Sure enough, when she opened her eyes on Saturday morning, welcome sunshine was pouring in their bedroom windows.

"I'm gonna see bears today," Susan said as soon as she woke up. Mandy was glad her little sister was happy about going to the zoo. Mama said the twins would never be able to sit still through a whole ball game.

"You're not leaving to go to the zoo until after lunch," Mandy informed her as she crawled out of bed. "We all have to pitch in and help clean house this morning."

Susan stopped and thought about that a minute. "It's a long time until lunch." She sounded a little disappointed.

For once Mandy agreed with Susan—it did seem like a long time. And she didn't like having to clean house when Lora and Caroline were both gone.

By the time Peter came home from the station at lunchtime,

though, John and Mandy were all ready to go. The three of them headed for the bus stop a few blocks from their house. As they waited, John and Peter started singing "Take Me Out to the Ball Game." Mandy looked around to see if anyone was within hearing distance.

Buy me some peanuts and Cracker Jacks.
I don't care if I never get back.

Then instead of being embarrassed, Mandy joined in until they were all laughing so hard they had tears in their eyes.

As they boarded the bus, Mandy made sure Peter sat between them. Without her sisters along, it was almost like having Peter all to herself. She didn't mind that as they bounced along, John and Peter talked on and on about Rainiers' players and the details of how they'd won the pennant last spring. Sitting there in the bus with the warm sun streaming in on her face, a warm glow of peace and contentment started at the top of her head and trickled all the way to her toes. She could have ridden that bus forever.

Since the ballpark was south of Yesler Way, the Mikimoto boys would catch another bus and meet them at the front gate. The gates hadn't opened when they stepped off the bus, but a noisy, happy crowd had already gathered.

"How'll we find Baiko and Dayu in all these people?" John asked.

"We'll find them," Peter promised. "Just as long as they wait by the gate, we'll find them." He closed his big hand over Mandy's. "Let's just make sure we don't get separated from one another."

Mandy felt safe and secure with Peter holding onto her.

"If we don't see them by the time we get to the turnstile," Peter said, "we'll just step aside and wait a few minutes."

As soon as the gates opened, the crowd moved quickly. When they approached the turnstiles, the boys were waiting for them.

"Wow," John said. "You must have camped here all night."

Baiko grinned. "Dayu here was determined we'd be the first ones in line."

Peter chuckled at their exuberance. "Come on, troops." He waved them forward like a scout leader. "Let's go to the ball game."

Mandy could nott remember a more wonderful day. She laughed and cheered and booed and shouted at the umpires right along with the boys. They downed hot dogs on soggy buns and ate boxes of sweet Cracker Jacks and drank ice-cold Nehi soda pop from drippy wet bottles. The dust in the air made John have one good coughing fit, but it didn't last long, and he seemed to be okay. If he coughed too much, they'd have to go home. Mandy wouldn't have liked that at all.

The Rainiers were strutting their stuff in this first home game of the season. By the top of the seventh, they were leading, seven to three. The boys were ready to take a trip to the rest room.

"You going with them?" Peter asked Mandy.

"Guess I better." She stood up and stretched her legs.

Peter tipped up his bottle of Nehi, draining the last, then said, "I'll stay here and fill you in on what happens."

"Great," John said. "Come on. I'll lead the way."

They filed down the stairs to the lower level. The boys went one way, and Mandy went the other. "Promise you'll wait for me right here," she said.

"Promise," Dayu told her.

She sure didn't want to have to find their seats by herself.

A few minutes later, when she came out of the cool, dark rest room area, Mandy squinted against the sunshine. Shading her eyes, she saw the boys standing at the stairs. They'd stationed themselves where they could watch the game and wait for her. As she moved toward them, she felt someone grab her arm.

"Hey, you," said a boy's voice.

Yanking her arm free, she whirled around to see two boys from John's class at school. One was Alex Brown, who had a curly mop of sandy hair. The other, Jim Hendricks, was a little shorter and dark complexioned.

"You're John McMichael's sister, right?" Alex asked, leaning toward her.

She nodded. These were the boys John played baseball with every recess. But they looked angry. "If you want to talk to him, he's right there." She pointed down the walkway toward John.

"We see him," Jim said through clenched teeth. "Him and his two Jap buddies."

Mandy bit her lip and stood stone-still, although she wanted to run away as fast as she could.

"We didn't know he was a Jap lover." Alex clenched and unclenched his fists. "He never told us his little secret."

Jim bumped her arm. "You tell him for us. Tell him we know. And tell him he'd better watch out. We're out to teach him a lesson."

They turned and walked away.

CHAPTER 12

John's Fight

Tears burned in Mandy's eyes as she stood there a moment. How could people be so hateful and mean? Those two boys sounded like the girls in the Golden Ring. She had no idea if she were going to tell John, or if she did, how and when she would do it.

For now, it was important to pretend nothing had happened. That would be hard because she was shaking from head to toe. John still hadn't seen her, so she slipped back into the rest room, splashed cold water on her face, and dried off on the linen towel, pulling it around and around until she found a clean place. Then she stopped and took a deep breath.

"Brother," John said when she stepped up beside them. "I wondered if you were gonna take all day."

"Yeah, we were about ready to send Dayu in to get you," Baiko said. They all giggled, Mandy included.

The Rainiers won their game, and Mandy tried to keep on cheering as she'd done before, but for her, the afternoon was spoiled. She couldn't stop thinking about the boys' threats. What were they planning to do to John?

Her silence at supper wasn't noticed. The twins were going on and on about the bears, elephants, and lions they'd seen. Ben could barely eat for demonstrating the roar of a lion. He even showed them how the elephants sucked peanuts up through their trunks. Mama kept telling him to calm down, but her warnings didn't faze him.

John described the winning home run, which was slammed with the bases loaded, bringing all the runners safely into home plate. Even Caroline had had a great day with her little charges and enjoyed telling stories of how cute and well behaved they were.

Meanwhile, Mandy was plotting a moment when she could privately tell John what had happened. After she and Caroline finished washing and drying the supper dishes, she went to her room to try to study for the quiz contest. She fluffed the pillows and propped herself up in her bed. On her lap was a fifth-grade language book that Miss LaFayette had let her borrow out of the library. Mandy was determined to learn the parts of speech and be able to identify them in sentences, but it was hard to keep her mind on her work. From down in the living room, she could hear the beginning of *Hit Parade* coming on the radio.

Just then, John passed by her door with Peter's small Silvertone radio in his hands, the electrical cord trailing behind him.

"John!" she called out.

He stopped and stuck his head in the door. "Yeah?"

"Where're you going?"

"Peter said I could borrow his radio tonight. He's gone riding with some of his friends. I'm going to listen to the programs I like, not the boring old *Hit Parade.*" He paused a minute. "Hey, want to take time out from your brain-strain to join me?"

She put aside the book and hopped up. "I'd love to." She

could learn the parts of speech Sunday afternoon.

He set the radio on his bedside table and got down on his hands and knees to locate the outlet.

"Rinso Blue gets your clothes white!" came the loud voice from the radio. John grabbed the dial to turn it down. "Don't need it that loud," he said with a grin.

As he was turning the dial from station to station, Mandy sat down on the rug beside him. "Did I tell you I saw two of your friends at the ball game?"

He turned around to look at her, a strange expression on his face. "You didn't say anything about it. Who'd you see?"

"Alex Brown and Jim Hendricks."

John swallowed hard. The radio was still giving out static since the station wasn't tuned in clearly. "Did they see me?"

She nodded.

"And?"

"They called you a Jap lover."

He turned back to the radio and busied himself with the dial. All of a sudden, the sounds of breaking glass and a police siren blared from the radio, followed by a burglar alarm, machine guns *rat-a-tat-tatting,* and tires squealing. They both jumped. It was the beginning of *Gangbusters.* John grabbed the knob to turn it down a little.

When he acted as though he were totally engrossed in the *Gangbusters* show, she added, "They said something else, John."

"Yeah?" He wouldn't look at her.

"They said they were going to teach you a lesson."

"Don't worry," he said. "I can take care of myself."

His voice didn't sound too sure. Mandy suddenly felt sorry

for him. He, too, had tried to fit in at Queen Anne, and now this. She could tell he didn't want to talk about it anymore, so she sat with him and they listened to all their favorite programs until time to go to bed.

The entire day was gone, and she hadn't studied at all. April 19 was drawing closer and closer. She wasn't sure if she was ready for the contest. How was she to know if she'd studied enough? At least the other kids had experienced the contest before. But to her it was all brand new.

In the night, she heard John coughing and heard Mama getting up with him. Mandy had heard Mama say once that his coughing always got worse when John became excited or upset. Mandy was sure John was upset over what she'd told him.

The sermon the next morning at church was taken from the Sermon on the Mount. When Pastor Martin talked about doing good to those who persecute you, Mandy thought about all the persecution against the Japanese in Baiko and Dayu's neighborhood. She thought of the persecution she'd received at school and the way Helga was treated. Even John's friends were mad at him simply because he was friends with two Japanese boys.

She didn't understand how you could always do good to people who said mean things to you. But then, Pastor Martin reminded them that Jesus knows that no one is capable of keeping all the instructions in the Bible.

"It was never God's plan for us to be good in and of ourselves," Pastor told his congregation. "That's why Jesus came and died. When we ask Jesus into our hearts, He not only brings the gift of salvation, He also equips us to follow His example and His instructions."

Mandy glanced over at John to see if he was listening. He was playing tic-tac-toe with Ben on the border of his Sunday school paper. It seemed to her that he really should be paying attention. This was pretty important stuff.

That night Mandy prayed for Jesus to help her be good to the girls in the Golden Ring and to help John be good to the boys who were angry at him.

Monday afternoon, Mandy was on the playground during recess and saw John sitting on top of the jungle gym all by himself. The ball game was going on without him. She wanted to go to him and tell him she knew how he felt, but that would only make it worse. He wouldn't want the boys to think he needed a girl to help him out.

Mandy was determined to stick close by John as they walked to and from school each day so she could see that nothing happened to him. For two days nothing happened at all. John was a little more glum than usual, but at least no one tried to hurt him. She was beginning to think Alex and Jim had made empty threats—that is, until Wednesday afternoon.

Mandy had stayed behind a minute to get another study book from Miss LaFayette. By the time she got outside, John was way ahead of her. As she was hurrying to catch up with him, she saw Alex and Jim step out in front of him on the sidewalk. Fear crawled over her in prickly waves. She wished Pastor Martin would appear to tell John how to be good to those bullies. She slowed down and tried to sneak around through front yards, crouching behind privet hedges.

When she came up to them, she heard Jim saying something like, "What do you have to say for yourself, Jap lover?"

"If I were you, I sure wouldn't be seen in public with them," Alex added.

"We don't like Jap lovers, do we, Alex?"

"No sir, Jack. We don't like 'em one little bit."

Peering through the hedge, Mandy could see they were moving closer to John. She didn't know whether to scream for help or run home to get Mama. Just then, Alex grabbed John's arms, and Jim reared back his fist for a hard punch.

A scream froze in Mandy's throat as she saw John convulse into a heavy coughing spasm. Then he went limp.

CHAPTER 13

Jujitsu

"Lay him flat," Mandy yelled as she jumped out from behind the hedge.

"We didn't do anything! Honest!" Alex said. His eyes were wide.

"Lay him out flat on his back," she ordered again. John's wheezing was punctuated by spasms of coughing. His face was growing redder by the minute.

The two did as she said, then they started to slip away. She stood up and glared at them. "Oh, no, you don't. You're both going to help me get him to the house. After he's rested a minute, that is."

"Not me," Jim said.

"Grab him and help," Alex ordered. "This was all your idea in the first place."

Mandy made them wait until John's breathing was back to normal. She'd seen Mama do the same thing plenty of times. Then she had them hook his arms over their shoulders. John just sort of stumbled along. When they were almost to the house, John realized what was going on. He shook the boys loose, and they took off like scared rabbits.

John turned to Mandy with a pained look. "You better not

tell Mama a word of this," he warned.

"You can trust me." She helped him the rest of the way up the walk. Mama met them at the door.

"What happened?" she demanded.

"Just a little coughing spell on the way home," Mandy told her.

Mama shook her head. "You were overdoing again, weren't you, John? I've told you again and again not to overdo. And we have no more of Mrs. Mikimoto's herbal tea."

She helped John into the living room and made him lie down on the couch. "Mandy, I'll call Mrs. Mikimoto, and you take the bus to go get it, just in case John has another attack in the night."

When Mama got off the phone, she said, "The boys will meet you in front of Walgreen's Drugstore at Fifth and Virginia."

Mandy knew that was right in the middle of downtown.

"She insisted that you not make the trip all the way to the Fairfax by yourself. And," Mama added, handing her money for the remedy, "make sure the boys take the money."

Mandy dropped the money into her pocket. She knew she could have made the trip to the hotel by herself. But Mrs. Mikimoto was so very polite.

She hurried to the bus stop and waited for the bus that said "Downtown" and "International District." As she stepped up in the front door, she saw Alex and Jim get on in the rear. She hurried and sat down, acting as though she hadn't noticed. So, the two scared rabbits hadn't run very far at all. How odd that they were on the same bus going the same direction. Were they following her? And if so, why?

Perhaps she shouldn't get off at the Walgreen's, after all. She'd get off a block sooner. But she'd never been downtown all by herself before. She didn't want to get lost.

While she was trying to figure out what to do, she saw Walgreen's Drugstore just down the street. And there were the Mikimoto brothers standing outside waiting for her. If she were Margo Lane on the *Green Hornet*, she'd know something terribly clever to do to get Jim and Alex off her trail. But she was just plain old Mandy McMichael, and she had no idea what to do.

When the bus stopped in front of Walgreen's, she stood up and got off. Glancing back, she saw Alex and Jim getting off as well. They were following her.

She ran up to Baiko and Dayu. Pushing the money into Dayu's hand, she grabbed the sack and blurted out, "Those two boys tried to beat up John. They followed me."

Just then, Alex yelled at them, "You Japs need to learn to stay in your own neighborhood."

"Quick," Baiko said to his brother. "To the alley!"

They dashed between the buildings with Mandy on their heels. Baiko went to the left, Dayu to the right. Mandy jumped behind Baiko. He was the bigger one.

She realized Jim and Alex weren't too smart when they both came running together right into the trap. Baiko grabbed one and Dayu the other. The Mikimoto boys were accomplished in jujitsu, having studied it for years. Before they knew what hit them, Jim and Alex were on their backs in the dirty alley.

"Come on, Mandy," Baiko said, grabbing her arm. "Let's get you to the bus stop."

"Will they be all right?" she asked, looking back over her

shoulder at the bewildered boys.

"We were gentle," Dayu assured her.

Stopping a moment, she called back to Jim and Alex, "My brother learned jujitsu from these boys. He'd have used it on you if he hadn't had a coughing attack."

Baiko chuckled as he hurried her back out to Fifth Street. "That's not really true," he said. "We taught John only a few moves."

"Close enough," she said, glancing back to see if they were still following.

Dayu saw her looking. "Don't worry, Mandy. They won't want another helping of that treatment anytime soon."

The bus for Queen Anne Hill was pulling up. The boys took her right up to the door. Mandy noticed the bus driver frown as he looked at the two Japanese boys.

If he only knew, she thought as she found her seat. Waving good-bye to her friends, she sat back and finally breathed a big sigh of relief. Wait until she told John what happened.

When she got home, John was asleep. After he awoke later that evening, Mama made sure he drank a big cup of the herbal tea, which he said tasted "worse than terrible." Then she insisted he go to bed early. That gave Mandy the opportunity to slip into his room and tell him the whole story.

He laughed as she described how Baiko and Dayu jumped and kicked and chopped before Jim and Alex knew what hit them.

"I wish I could have seen it. Tell me again."

Mother had instructed John to lie down and stay still, but he was propped up in bed, soaking up Mandy's every word.

She described the scene all over again.

"I can't believe they'd follow you. Can they really hate the Japanese that much?"

"I don't know." Then she wondered, could the Golden Ring really hate her and Helga as much as they did?

"There's one other thing I haven't told you yet," she said, grinning.

"What?"

"I told Jim and Alex that you knew jujitsu."

"You didn't." He smiled. "Did you really?"

"It wasn't really a lie. You know some, don't you?"

"Some," he agreed. He thought about that a minute. "I may go to the Mikimotos' on Saturday. I could use a refresher. I never thought I'd need it before this." He took one of his pillows, fluffed it, and repositioned it. "I wouldn't ever want to hurt anyone, but maybe I could get the other boys' respect this way."

Mandy thought about that a minute. "I think we get respect by just being ourselves."

"I suppose so." Then John added, "I feel really bad that Baiko and Dayu fought my battle for me. When the guys at school talk about how awful the Japanese are, I don't say one word in their defense." He shook his head. "That's just not right."

Mandy didn't know what to say to him. She knew how hard it was to take a stand when everyone was against you. "Pastor Martin said that Jesus could equip us to do the things we're supposed to do."

John nodded. "Yeah, I know. I heard him."

She didn't see how he could have heard when he was playing tic-tac-toe, but she didn't argue. "Well?"

"Well what?"

"How about if we pray together?" She could tell John was a little embarrassed. They'd often prayed as a family, but never just the two of them.

"You go ahead," he said.

"Bow your head," she told him. As they bowed their heads, she asked Jesus to equip both of them to do what He wanted them to do at school.

As she opened her eyes, she noticed how tired John looked. "You'd better get to sleep, or Mama will kill both of us."

He nodded in agreement. That proved how tired he was. And he was missing *Jack Armstrong, All-American Boy* on the radio. That really proved how tired he was.

She tiptoed out and went to her room to study.

Much to her surprise, by the time Mandy had made perfect scores on the Wednesday spelling test three times in a row, no one said a word about it. She could hardly believe it. She still wasn't included, but at least no one was nagging at her all the time. And she loved her two afternoons a week with Miss LaFayette.

The librarian was becoming a good friend. They discussed their favorite authors and told why they liked certain story plots better than others. Miss LaFayette even explained to Mandy what was required at college to become a librarian. Mandy thought that would be the greatest job in the whole world.

Each week, Miss LaFayette trusted her with more and more responsibility. She surprised Mandy one afternoon by telling her she could be the story-reader in the first-grade classroom that afternoon. The first-graders seemed to enjoy having Mandy in their classroom, but she was the one who had the most fun!

A week after the incident with Jim and Alex, Mandy and John were walking home from school together.

"You'll never guess what happened today," John said. He was smiling.

"Tell me."

"As usual, the guys were going on and on again about how awful the Japanese were, and as simple as you please, I said, 'They're like any other group of people in the world. Some are good and some are bad.'"

"John. Did you really?"

"I sure did. Know what I said then?"

"What?"

"I said, 'Even Kato, the housekeeper on *Green Hornet,* is Japanese. And he's a good person.'"

"What did they say to that?"

"They said they guessed that was right. One of the guys pointed out that the Japanese who are attacking China are awful bad. I agreed with him, and then I said, 'But I bet not all the people who live in Japan agree with what they're doing—and not all the ones in Seattle agree, either.'"

"I'm so proud of you, John. Really proud of you."

"Thanks." He grinned at her.

"Did Jim or Alex say anything?"

He nodded. "Alex said that the Japanese invented the art of jujitsu and that it was a swell form of self-defense."

Mandy laughed.

Then John said softly, "I'm sure glad you suggested we pray."

CHAPTER 14

In the Limelight

Spring seemed to woo Mandy outdoors, and she had to admit that Queen Anne Hill was a beautiful place. Much more beautiful than the International District. She loved to go rollerskating near their house.

But getting off by herself was next to impossible these days. With Caroline taking on more baby-sitting jobs and Lora gone so much, Mandy became the catch-all girl. She was either keeping an eye on the twins or helping Mama cook, clean, and iron. Sometimes Mandy raised a fuss and told Mama that John could watch the twins as well as she could. It seemed to her that John got off scot-free from everything.

Of course, that wasn't completely true because Dad made him wash the car, mow the lawn, and keep the garage clean. But that didn't take him very long at all.

On the Saturday afternoon before the quiz contest, Mandy asked permission to skate to Kinnear Park. It took a minute to get Mama's attention. The Mixmaster was whirring away as she mixed up a chocolate cake for supper. Mama turned it off and cleaned the beaters with a rubber spatula. Miraculously, the twins were nowhere in sight, so Mama handed Mandy a beater to lick.

As she cleaned off the last bit of chocolate batter, Mandy

asked again if she could skate to the park.

"Kinnear Park?" Mama asked. "All by yourself?"

Mandy wanted to remind her that John went all over the neighborhood by himself on his bicycle, but she was afraid Mama would remind her that John was a boy and two years older.

"Yes, all by myself." She held up a science book. "I'd like to be able to study this before next Friday."

Mama raised her eyebrows. "Is the contest that close? My, how time flies." She wiped her hands on her apron and proceeded to grease the cake pans, lining them with waxed paper so the cake wouldn't stick. "It's Friday afternoon at two, right?"

Mandy nodded. She knew Mama planned to be there. "And I sure need to study."

"Yes, I suppose you do. I'm proud of you, Mandy. You've made such an improvement in your grades." She poured the batter into the pans, scraping out the last bit with the spatula. "I suppose you do need time alone." The bowl clinked as she set it down on the white enamel cabinet. "Oh, all right. But just for an hour. I suppose John can play with the twins for a while."

"Thank you, Mama." Mandy gave her mother a quick hug and ran to get her skates.

As she sat on the porch, tightening the skates on her shoes with her skate key, she said to the twins, "A cake bowl's sitting in on the counter waiting to be licked clean." While they ran inside, she grabbed her book and skated off as fast as she could.

It was a glorious day. The mist that had hung heavy that morning had lifted, and the sun beamed through the trees, making dappled patches in her path as she skated down the sidewalk toward the park.

She decided to go to the far side of the park, where she could find a spot that overlooked the sparkling waters of Elliott Bay. People were everywhere, walking, bicycling, skating, and pushing baby buggies. Cars stopped, and families lugged out their picnic baskets, looking around for vacant picnic tables.

Mandy sat on a park bench and took off her skates, made her way to a shade tree near a lily pond, and sat down to read the science book. In the distance, the bay spread out before her. Perfect! No sisters or brothers anywhere. Of course, she would have loved to have had Peter come along. If he'd been there, he'd be reading a book as well.

As the afternoon sun moved across the sky, she got up periodically and moved with the shade. Every once in a while, she glanced up to look around at the people strolling by. At one point, a flash of red made her look off to her left. It was the unmistakable red cardigan belonging to Helga Gottman and the unmistakable roll-step walk. Helga walked up to the rock ledge that surrounded the pool and sat down. She sat there for a time, staring into the water.

Mandy wondered if the girl lived near the park. What a perfect opportunity this would be to talk to her and learn more about her. With no Golden Ring nearby to spoil things, maybe Mandy could reach out and be a friend to Helga.

Lifting her strapped-together skates over her shoulder and grabbing her book, Mandy stood up and walked toward the other girl. As she approached, she smiled and said, "Hello, Helga."

The girl looked up at her, startled.

"I didn't mean to scare you. Do you come here often?" Mandy turned and pointed back up the hill. "I live up that way about five or six blocks. That is, I think they're blocks. All the streets are so curvy in this neighborhood."

As she was talking along in her most friendly voice, Helga stood up and simply walked off. Step-roll, step-roll, step-roll down the path toward the sidewalk.

Mandy stared after her. Such rudeness! Here she was trying her best to be nice, and the girl just walked away. Well, Helga Gottman could just go on being lonely for all she cared. Mandy asked an elderly man sitting on a park bench what time it was and found out it was time to go home anyway.

Mandy had been in a spelling bee in third grade, so she knew a little bit about being asked questions in front of others. But the morning of the quiz contest, her stomach churned so she could hardly bear to watch John eating his Wheaties. She didn't even care that he got the brand-new Jack Armstrong decoder badge out of the box.

Throughout the day, the tension grew until she felt she might burst wide open. She kept taking deep breaths, but that didn't help. Would she freeze when she stepped up on the stage? Would her brain short-circuit because she was so tense? Answering Caroline's questions in the bedroom was much different than being on a stage with the whole school watching. Whatever possessed her to think she could do this? Only a few fourth-graders even signed up. Most of the entrants were fifth- and sixth-graders. What chance did she have?

The twins were oblivious as they walked home for lunch, running along and laughing and acting silly. At the house,

Mandy told her mother she couldn't eat a bite, but Mama insisted she at least eat an apple. "It's light," she said. "And you need something in your stomach."

Mandy forced down the apple, reading a history book as she ate, then hurried back to school. The contest was to begin at two o'clock. The hands on the classroom pendulum clock barely moved for an entire hour.

When Mrs. Crowley said it was time for those who had entered the contest to be dismissed to go to the auditorium, Mandy wasn't sure her legs would carry her. She felt weak all over. Perhaps she would faint dead away, and she wouldn't have to worry about the contest at all.

Four long rows of chairs were arranged on the stage for the participants. Mandy glanced around at the others, but no one appeared to be as nervous as she was. She sat down and folded her damp, clammy hands in her lap. Then, reaching in her pocket, she pulled out her flowered handkerchief and began to twist the corner of it. That gave her hands something to do.

Mama and the twins slipped in the rear door and took seats near the back of the room. Susan gave a shy little wave. Students began filing in, and Mandy saw John come in and take his seat. She knew he was rooting for her.

Within a few minutes, the entire auditorium was packed, and the principal stepped to the lectern to give the welcome address. He explained the rules, saying that each student, when asked a question, must stand to answer. If he or she failed to answer correctly in the designated time, that person must leave the stage and take a seat down front.

"The teacher asking the questions will indicate the category," he continued, "whether arithmetic, science, history, or language. We've attempted to include an equal mix. This contest is for the versatile student. The well-read student."

As he said that, Mandy happened to catch Miss LaFayette's eye. The librarian smiled at her. That smile bolstered Mandy's courage.

Then the questions began. Mr. Cutts, the sixth-grade teacher, called out, "Mandy McMichael." She jumped to her feet. Her chair scooted and made a clattering noise on the floor. There were a few snickers. She felt her face flush.

"The category is language," he said, paying no attention to her clumsiness. "In this sentence, 'Johnny climbed up the hill,' what part of speech is the word *climbed?*"

Mandy swallowed hard. How she wished she could have a glass of water. "The word *climbed* is a verb."

"Correct," said Mr. Cutts. "You may be seated."

As she sat down, she released a deep sigh. She'd done it. She'd actually answered the first question, and she was still in.

Three of the students were out on the very first round.

On the second round, her question was history. Mr. Cutts cleared his throat. "Give the date when Fort Sumter fell into Confederate hands," he said. Then he added, "Give the day, month, and year."

Mandy closed her eyes and forced herself to breathe deeply. "April," she said. "April 12, 1861."

"Correct," Mr. Cutts said, smiling, and Mandy sat back down.

Her biggest fear was a word problem in math. For some reason, figures didn't compute as quickly in her head as facts.

A sixth-grade boy named Dennis Lynch, who, according to

John, was one of the smartest boys in his class, moved over beside her as empty chairs were taken from the stage. As he did, he looked over at her and smiled. He didn't seem a bit nervous. They were competing against one another, yet he smiled at her. His smile seemed to say, "Enjoy yourself. This is fun."

She smiled back at him. As she did, strangely enough, the agonizing tightness in her chest eased up. Between questions, she'd been staring hard at the floor in front of her feet. Now she allowed herself to look out over the crowd. Suddenly, it occurred to her that there was nothing to be nervous about. Or to be afraid of. So what if she got a word problem and it was hard? So what if she missed it? She'd come this far, and there would always be next year. She was up there doing her very best, and that was all that mattered.

There were seven students left on the stage when she received her first word problem. "If three girls each had a basket containing a dozen oranges, and they wanted to give nine friends an equal number of oranges, how many oranges would each friend receive?"

Mandy began to figure in her head. She had only a few minutes. *Three dozen oranges would be thirty-six, divided by nine.* "Each friend would receive four oranges," she said.

"Correct," said Mr. Cutts.

When she sat down, she heard Dennis whisper, "Good job, fourth-grader."

By now her nervousness had transformed into exhilaration. She truly was having fun! So when she and Dennis were the only students left on the stage, she felt as though the two of them shared a private joke.

"Dennis Lynch."

Dennis stood to his feet.

"The category is history. Give the date when King John sealed the Magna Carta at Runnymede."

"King John sealed the Magna Carta on June 15, 1225."

"That is not correct," Mr. Cutts said.

Dennis sat down. And he was still smiling. Mandy wondered if maybe he already had a set of encyclopedias at his house. According to the rules, if she missed the question as well, he would be given yet another question, and the contest would continue.

As her name was called, she stood. The question was repeated. But she knew. The year wasn't 1225. It was 1215.

As soon as she gave the correct answer and Mr. Cutts said, "Correct," the entire auditorium burst into loud applause. Dennis shook her hand and congratulated her, telling her what a good job she'd done. Mr. Cutts patted her back. Miss LaFayette hugged her. John came up on stage to tell her how proud he was of her. Mother was there, and the twins were bouncing around her like two little jack-in-the-boxes.

"Mandy won! Mandy won!" they chanted. And Mama didn't tell them to hush.

Even old Mrs. Crowley was on the stage fussing over her.

When everything had calmed down, Mr. Cutts announced that the set of encyclopedias would be delivered to the McMichael home the following week. Then he said, "This is the first time in the history of the quiz contest that a fourth-grader has won."

Applause echoed through the auditorium. Mandy couldn't

remember ever being so happy.

Since it was time for school to be dismissed, the building emptied quickly. Mama and the twins waited in the front hall while Mandy went to her classroom to get her books and jacket. When she came out of the room, Jane Stevens was standing in the hall almost as though she were waiting for Mandy.

Mandy started to walk right past her. After all, no one in the Golden Ring had ever spoken to her except to torment her.

But Jane said, "Mandy?"

Mandy stopped and looked at her.

"I just wanted to tell you I think you did a swell job. I would have been scared spitless up there." The girl gave a weak smile.

"Thank you, Jane. It's nice of you to say so. I was pretty scared at first."

"I just wanted you to know. . . ." She stopped a minute. "I'm glad you didn't let what the girls. . ." Catching herself, she began again. "I'm glad you didn't let what we said stop you."

She left without another word.

CHAPTER 15

Summertime

Every time Mandy walked through their living room and saw the beautiful encyclopedia set with its embossed burgundy covers, she wanted to burst with pride. She told everyone in the family that they were welcome to use the books at any time. "Just make sure you put them back where they belong, and don't handle them with dirty hands."

The evening after the contest, Mama let them all stay up until Dad arrived home. They were all in the kitchen when he arrived, and together they had a celebration in Mandy's honor. Dad looked tired, but she could tell he was very happy.

"Mandy, I don't know what happened to cause you to care about your studies again," he said, "but whatever it was, I'm so grateful."

After that, the school year was a breeze. Other kids began to talk to her. Even Dennis smiled and said hello when they passed in the hallways and saw one another out on the playground. While Elizabeth wasn't at all polite, she stopped attacking Mandy.

Now if someone called her Mandy Einstein, it didn't sound like an insult. It sounded like a compliment, and people smiled when they said it.

Each evening, Mama listened closely to Edward R. Murrow's news reports. As a European correspondent, Murrow gave the news right on the spot. The news in May was not good. All of Holland had been overrun by the Nazis in four short days. Belgium was taken almost as quickly.

"Like little dominoes," Mama said. She kept her chair close to the big console radio in the living room and listened as she knitted blankets and clothing for those in need who were in the midst of war.

School came to an end, and the wonderful, happy, carefree days of summer arrived. John built a wagon for the twins. He tied it to his bicycle, and with Mandy on her skates, the four of them traveled throughout the neighborhood. John spent hours in the backyard practicing the new jujitsu moves that Baiko and Dayu had taught him. In turn, he tried to teach them to Ben.

Mama let them go to the drugstore for candy and double-dip ice cream cones, which dripped sticky drops on them all the way home. And Saturday movie matinees became part of every week.

That first Saturday in June, they went to see a Gene Autry Western. The twins liked Gene Autry. Mandy's favorite Western star was Roy Rogers. John liked Tom Mix because Tom just "chased the bad guys and didn't stop to sing songs."

But first there was the Movietone newsreel, and that's where they learned about the evacuation from Dunkirk, France. The film showed British soldiers who had been trying to keep Germany from invading France running away from Hitler's army. The British government sent anything that could float across the

English Channel to bring their soldiers home. Mandy watched ordinary citizens risk their lives to get destroyers, tugs, cross-channel packets, paddlewheel ferries, fishing boats, yachts, and dinghies across the water. Many made the trip again and again.

"When the evacuation was over," said the booming voice, "more than three hundred thousand men had been carried to safety. While it was a triumph of undaunting human spirit, it is at the same time a military disaster."

Mandy knew from what she'd heard Mama and Dad saying that France now stood totally alone in Europe. Could they hold Hitler at bay? The world would find out soon enough.

A couple weeks later, Mandy came into the living room to see her mother weeping. "Mama," she said, hurrying over to her chair. "What is it? It's not Mark, is it?"

Mama dabbed at her cheeks with a handkerchief and shook her head. "France stood so strong through the Great War. She sacrificed so many of her sons. And now she's fallen. It's a sad day in history, Mandy. A very sad day for a glorious people."

Mandy didn't know what to make of it all. Even Italy, whom most Americans felt would side with the Allies, had declared war on both Britain and France earlier in the month. Was there a country in the world that wasn't at war?

And then there was the election coming that fall. Dad and Mama and Peter and Lora discussed it at length whenever the four of them were together—usually on Saturday nights and Sunday afternoons. No one knew for sure what President Roosevelt's plans were. Would he run for office for a third term?

No president in history had ever served for three full terms. It was unheard of.

"I'm sure he must be weary," Mama said, her knitting needles clicking in rhythm. A fan by the window was moving the warm, humid air around the living room.

"Yes," Dad agreed. "But changing horses in the middle of the stream could be disastrous. We desperately need his leadership now."

Mandy and Susan were lying on the living room floor as Mandy helped Susan cut out her new Shirley Temple paper dolls from the paper doll book. Susan had already accidentally cut off the pant leg of one of the cute ski outfits, so she'd asked Mandy to help. At Dad's words, Susan looked up.

"Where's the horse, Dad?" she asked.

"It's just a figure of speech, Susan," Mandy explained. "There's not really any horse."

"Good leadership is always necessary for a country like ours," Dad went on, "but at a time like this, it's vital. We need Roosevelt just like Britain needs Churchill."

At the next Saturday matinee, Mandy saw film clips of Hitler standing outside the railway carriage where he'd forced France's officials to surrender. More than a million French, the narrator said, had been taken as prisoners. Mandy couldn't picture a million people—especially not as prisoners. It was just too awful to comprehend.

"We helped the French in the last war," John said that evening at supper, "why don't we help them now?"

Mandy wondered the same thing. Couldn't someone do something to help?

Mama shook her head. "It's not that simple, I'm afraid."

"You see, John," Peter spoke up, "war is a terrible thing. It costs a great deal of money, and more than that, it costs lives. Many Americans feel that the war in Europe is none of our business. They think we should stay out of it."

"But will Hitler allow us to keep minding our own business?" John asked.

"That, my dear brother," Peter said, slapping John on the shoulder, "is a very, very good question. One I hope Congress will soon address."

Dad and Mama both seemed to breathe a little easier when they learned that Roosevelt had agreed to run again. At the Democratic convention in July, he was nominated on the very first ballot. And because her parents were pleased, Mandy was pleased as well.

Several times during the summer, when Mandy was able to slip away to Kinnear Park to be alone and read, she'd see Helga. But she made no attempt to be friendly to the girl. She didn't even wave. Helga sometimes glanced in her direction. Mandy would look at her, then look back at her book and keep on reading. If Helga didn't want to be friends, there was nothing Mandy could do about it.

One afternoon as Mandy was strapping on her skates, a voice from behind her said, "You dropped this."

Helga was holding out the special bookmark that Miss LaFayette had given Mandy. It was a gift for having won the quiz contest.

"Thank you, Helga. I wouldn't have wanted to lose that. It's special to me."

Helga nodded. "I thought so. Miss LaFayette likes you a lot."

Mandy didn't know what to say to that. She put the book-mark in her library book and strapped on her other skate. Just then it occurred to her that Helga would never be able to skate. It was a sad thought. No one probably had any idea how much this girl suffered because she was lame.

Mandy determined to try once again to be nice. But when she looked up, Helga was gone. Shaking her head, she wondered if it had been this hard for King David to get to know Mephibosheth.

CHAPTER 16
Helga's Visit

When Mandy opened her eyes, it was still dark. What had awakened her? she wondered. She punched at her pillow, turned over, and tried to go back to sleep. There it was again. Whimpering. Mandy sat up in bed and looked over at Susan. Her little sister was kicking and whimpering in her sleep.

Mandy slipped out of bed and stepped over to her sister's bed. "Susan," she said softly. Then she lay her hand on her sister's shoulder. "Susan, honey, what's the matter? Are you having a dream?"

Susan roused a little. "A bad dream," she said.

"Here's your Shirley Temple doll." Mandy picked up the doll from the floor and put it in Susan's waiting arms.

Susan mumbled her thanks and went back to sleep.

The bad dreams came several times over the next few nights. Finally Mandy felt she should tell Mama about it.

"It's those movies you children have been seeing," was Mama's explanation. "I probably shouldn't let the little ones go with you."

Mandy had to admit the newsreels had been pretty scary lately. But when Mama said something about the twins not going to the movies every Saturday, they pitched such a fit, she decided to relent.

Mandy talked with Susan, trying to find out if something was bothering her, but Susan just shrugged her little shoulders and said everything was all right. Mandy wished she knew how to help her little sister stop having nightmares.

One afternoon when John was in the backyard practicing jujitsu with Ben, Mandy asked Susan if she'd like to walk to the park, just the two of them. Susan's eyes lit up.

"I sure would," she said

After getting Mama's permission, they were on their way. Susan held tightly to Mandy's hand as they walked up one hill and down another until they reached Kinnear Park. Mandy took her sister to the playground, where they played on the slippery slide and swings until they were hot and sweaty.

They bought cones of sweetened shaved ice from the sidewalk vendor and took them to the lily pond. There they ate the refreshing treat and watched the shiny goldfish. The paper cones got all soggy before they were half finished with them. Susan's had a little leak in the bottom, trailing red drips down the front of her playsuit. After Susan drank the very last drops, Mandy took the cups to the trashcan. When she came back to where Susan was sitting, Helga was looking at them.

"You don't have a book," she said to Mandy.

It was like a statement and a question all mixed together. "No, I don't. I came to play with Susan." Motioning to Susan, she said, "This is my little sister, Susan."

Helga nodded. "I saw you walk her home from school every day at lunch."

"Oh yeah. I guess you did." Turning to Susan, she said, "Susan, this is one of my classmates. Her name is Helga Gottman."

Susan looked up and said, "Hi, Helga. Sit down with us. Want to?"

And Helga did.

Making conversation with Helga was not an easy job, but at least Mandy learned more than she'd ever known before.

"My grandpa was here before any of these fancy people," Helga said, waving her hand in the air as though to take in all of Queen Anne Hill. "He says we were first. We were first."

Mandy wasn't sure what to say, but Susan piped up and said, "We just came last year. So we're sort of new."

"I'm not new here," Helga said. "I've lived here ever since I was born."

"Do you live with your grandfather?" Mandy asked.

Helga nodded. "I live with Grandpa."

"Where are your parents?"

"Dead," she said. And that was that. She got up to leave.

"Come by to see us at our house sometime," Susan said.

"Yes, Helga," Mandy added. "Come for a visit." She called out the address, but Helga walked away without looking back.

An orphan. Helga was as alone as Little Orphan Annie in the funny papers. Only she didn't have any Daddy Warbucks. Or even a nice dog named Sandy.

"Thank you for taking me to the park," Susan said to Mandy as they walked back home. "I like being with you."

"You're welcome, Susan."

Later, Mandy thought about what Susan had said. It sounded like something she would have said to Peter or Lora. She loved to be with them and have them pay attention to her. But both of them were so busy. Lora was hardly ever at home anymore. And Peter was either working or studying. It never occurred to Mandy that Susan might feel left out as well. Had her little sister needed her when she had her nose stuck in a book all the time? Or when she tried to get off by herself?

Perhaps being with Susan wasn't like being the baby of the family after all. Perhaps it was time for Mandy to take her place in the family as Susan's older sister.

The next time Susan had a nightmare, she mumbled words instead of just kicking the covers. Mandy hurried over to see if she could make any sense of the mumbling. She sat on the edge of Susan's bed and leaned her head down close. The words sounded like, "I don't know. I don't know how. It's too hard." Then she started whimpering.

"What's too hard, Susan? Tell Mandy. What's too hard?"

In the dim glow of the night-light, she saw Susan's eyes flutter open. Then she sat up and threw her arms around Mandy's neck, clinging to her so tightly, Mandy thought she was going to be choked. "I don't wanna go," she wailed pitifully.

"Wait, wait a minute." With Susan still clinging to her neck, Mandy lifted her little sister so she could reach the lamp on the bedside table. "Wake up, Susan. Tell me what you were dreaming about."

Susan let go of Mandy's neck and rubbed her eyes with her fists. She looked up at Mandy. "I had a dream."

"I know. A bad dream. Now tell me what it was about."

Snuggling close to Mandy, she said, "Don't make me have to go to first grade, Mandy. I'm scared."

Mandy buried her face in Susan's soft curls. "Now, how can a big girl like you be scared of school?" she asked. "That's the strangest thing I've ever heard of." She leaned back and looked at Susan's worry-filled little face. "You've already been in school for a whole year. Why are you afraid now?"

Mandy remembered a year ago when Susan was dancing all over the room in her excitement to go to kindergarten. Mandy was the one who had been afraid and dreaded going.

"That was kindergarten." Susan reached over and pulled Shirley Temple onto her lap. "All we do in kindergarten is play. First grade is real hard. I don't even know how to read."

Mandy shook her head. So that was what was causing the bad dreams. "Who told you first grade was so hard?"

"Mary."

"And who is Mary?"

"A girl in my kindergarten class."

Mandy put her arm around Susan and pulled her close. "If Mary was in kindergarten with you, how does she know about first grade?"

Susan shrugged. "I dunno."

"She doesn't know. But I do, because I've been in first grade. And I can tell you that you will do fine."

"Are you sure?"

"Sure I'm sure. Would I lie to my favorite little sister?"

Susan laughed. "I'm your only little sister."

"Tell you what. Tomorrow you and I will get a storybook, and I'll show you some words and tell you what the letters are. Would you like that?"

"You hear that, Shirley Temple?" Susan said to the doll in her lap. "Mandy's gonna help me learn to read."

"Now you lie down and go back to sleep." Mandy leaned

down and kissed her sister's face. "Everything's going to be all right. G'night, honey."

" 'Night, Mandy."

"Our Gal Sunday," the radio announcer said, "the story of an orphan girl named Sunday from the little mining town of Silver Creek, Colorado. . ."

Mama turned the radio up a little. Mandy knew this was one of her favorite shows. Mandy was putting the iron and ironing board away. The twins had had their lunch, and Mama had put them down for a nap. Mandy was glad the ironing was finished. It was too hot to iron. Peter was asleep on the couch. He'd had a wisdom tooth extracted that morning, so his boss told him to stay home. Mama had tried her best to keep everyone quiet so he could rest.

"The story that asks the question," the announcer of *Our Gal Sunday* went on, "can this girl from a mining town in the West find happiness as the wife of a wealthy and titled Englishman, Lord Henry Brinthrope?"

Mandy knew there was never going to be an answer to that question. If the question were answered, the show would be over.

Just then, a knock sounded at the front door. Mandy hurried to answer it before the noise woke Peter. To her surprise, Helga stood at the door. "I came to visit," the girl said in her raspy voice. "Like you said."

CHAPTER 17

New Friends

Mandy stood at the door dumbfounded. What was she supposed to say? Or do? Helga evidently had no idea it was not polite to drop in for a visit without phoning first.

"Hello, Helga. Won't you come in? It's good to see you."

She led Helga into the kitchen. "Mother," she said, "this is Helga Gottman. From school."

"Welcome, Helga. I remember seeing you at school." Mandy could tell by the look on Mama's face that she was thinking back. "At the Christmas program, I believe it was."

Mandy winced. Why did her mother have to mention the Christmas program, of all things? But to her surprise, Helga smiled. Mandy hadn't seen the girl smile very often.

"The program," she said, "when I fell down."

"Oh, yes." Mother laughed. "That's right. I believe both of you took a tumble that night." She folded a damp dish towel and hung it over the rods above the sink. "The twins are napping in my bedroom, Mandy. Why don't you take Helga to your room?"

Mandy wasn't sure what she was going to do once they got to her room. Never had she felt so awkward. She led the way upstairs and down the hallway toward her room. "My older sisters' room is here," she said, waving a hand in that direction.

"And Susan and I are right in here."

"Pretty," Helga said as she stepped inside. "Your room is pretty." She looked around. "Do you have your own radio?"

Mandy shook her head. "Only Peter has his own. His room is down at the end. Sometimes if there's something real special on, I can ask permission to take the one from the kitchen and bring it up here."

Helga nodded but said nothing. She walked over to the dressing table and sat down, looking at the items there. She picked up a couple bobby pins out of the plastic dish where Mandy kept them.

Glancing at Helga's hair, which was never fixed properly, Mandy said, "Want me to show you how to put your hair up in pin curls?"

Helga jumped up from the tufted stool and walked to the door. "You want to make me different?" she said. She strode out into the hallway, and Mandy hurried after her, bewildered. "That's what Elizabeth Barrington would do. Change me. Make me different."

As Mandy followed her down the stairs, she realized she had a lot to learn about Helga Gottman. And it was going to take a lot of time.

At the bottom of the stairs, Helga suddenly stopped. "Where are the encyclopedias?"

Forgetting that Peter was resting, Mandy pointed to the living room. "In there."

Without asking, Helga walked in the room and looked at the books sitting on the shelf. Peter opened one eye to see what the disturbance was, readjusted the ice pack on his face, and said nothing.

Mandy stepped up beside Helga. "If it hadn't been for you, I would never have won these."

"I know," the girl replied.

"Thank you for saying what you did that day in the library."

"It was the truth." Helga turned back to the hallway and headed in her roll-step gait to the front door.

Not waiting for Mandy to open the door, she let herself out. Going down the sidewalk, Helga called, "I'll come back again."

That evening at supper, Mama told the story about Helga coming to visit, unannounced. Mandy could tell by Mama's tone that she hadn't minded one bit. "That girl may be a little slow in speech and in her ways," Mama said, "but she's certainly not dumb."

Mandy thought that was a good description. "God loves her just like King David loved Mephibosheth."

"Who?" John asked, laying down the pork chop he'd been de-vouring. "Who in the world is Mephibo. . . Whatever you said."

"If you'd listen in church, you'd know." She explained about Mephibosheth and how King David hunted for him throughout the land and then gave him a place at the king's table.

Peter, who was eating a clear soup instead of pork chops, said, "Hey, little sis. I'm proud of you." Putting down his spoon, he got up from his place to come over and give her a hug.

"But I didn't do anything," she said.

"I saw you with Helga," he said. "How kind you were with her. So in a way you're right—it really isn't what you do, it's who you are. And you are one sweet girl." Before sitting back down, he gave her another hug.

Mandy basked in his praise. It made her feel all grown up.

She'd gained something that was far better than a piggyback ride—she'd gained her older brother's respect.

Each evening out on the porch swing, Mandy read to Susan from *The Bobbsey Twins in the Country*. Susan especially liked the book because there were two sets of twins in the family. Freddie and Flossie were the two younger ones, and Nan and Bert were the two older ones.

Mandy read slowly and pointed out words and named letters. By the time they were finished with the book, Susan was saying, "T-w-i-n-s. That spells twins. I can read and spell both." Of course, she couldn't really read. Not yet anyway. But that wasn't important. What mattered was that the nightmares had ceased. Mandy never realized before how little it took to make her sister happy.

Money wasn't as tight as it had been the previous school year, so Mandy had three new dresses with which to begin school. And a few new skirts and blouses as well. And, of course, her dungarees.

John would be going to junior high and would no longer be walking to school with her each day. She'd miss that. But she knew she'd be all right this year.

Before the first day, she told Mama she'd need lunch money.

Mama's eyebrows went up. "Oh, really? You're not coming home for lunch this year?"

Mandy shook her head. "The twins will be at school all day, so there's no need for me to walk home. I may just as well stay there, too."

Mama nodded. "My goodness. All of my children in school all day. I won't know what to do with myself."

Mandy didn't believe that for a minute.

When Mandy walked into the fifth-grade classroom, she looked around at the familiar faces and felt right at home. Mrs. Patterson, their teacher, was a bright-eyed lady whom Mandy knew would be much more on top of things than Mrs. Crowley ever was. Mrs. Crowley, she soon learned, had retired and would not be back. That was good news for this year's fourth-graders.

Elizabeth Barrington was in the center of her friends, the same as always. She was bronzed with a summer tan, and her honey-hair was more golden than ever. Someone said she'd spent the summer traveling with her parents.

And, of course, Helga appeared wearing her frayed red cardigan. She actually smiled at Mandy when she walked in the door. Amazing.

When the day got underway, Mrs. Patterson made various announcements. One important announcement was that Miss Bowen had joined the Red Cross. "So," Mrs. Patterson added, "since the school has been unable to hire a new physical education instructor, we'll have regular recess this year."

The class broke into a spontaneous cheer.

Mrs. Patterson put her finger over her mouth. "Shh. No talking aloud without raising our hands first."

It was going to be a very good year.

As soon as Mandy could do so, she hurried to the library to see Miss LaFayette. She had some unfinished business about a lie she had told. Now she could tell the truth about the torn book, and it would no longer be like tattling. Miss LaFayette gave her a hug and said she forgave her for the lie, and Mandy felt a load go off her shoulders. She'd carried that weight around for much too long.

School had been in session only a few days when the terrible news broke of Germany bombing London. Nearly a thousand bombers struck at the heart of the great city. No one could believe it. Killing innocent civilians on purpose—that was unheard of.

"This, if anything," Mandy's father said, "will raise the sympathies of the people of the United States for the Brits."

On the newsreels, Mandy saw young schoolchildren hiding in trenches while the battle raged overhead. She saw the British loading their children onto trains to send them into the countryside to live with other families until the Blitz, as the bombing was called, was over.

The terrifying Battle of Britain dragged on through the autumn. Many people, including her teacher, Mrs. Patterson, said they didn't see how Britain could hold on much longer. But the Brits did hold on. And their prime minister, Winston Churchill, said it was England's "finest hour."

"It's the Royal Air Force," Dad kept saying with a distinct note of pride in his voice. "I've always said it's the airplanes that will win this war. We need to be making more of them."

Mandy wasn't exactly sure what Dad did every day, working long hours at the Boeing plant, but she was confident he had a part in helping Britain shoot down the German planes and protect and defend their homeland. And she was immensely proud of him.

Some days Helga sat with her during lunch. Some days she didn't. That's the way Helga was. Mandy was trying to learn to appreciate her new friend's ups and downs—and not try to change her. Though Mandy was nothing like King David, she still felt as though she were allowing Mephibosheth the privilege of sitting at the table. Perhaps someday she'd be able to tell Helga about how much Jesus, the real King, loved her.

Two girls in fifth grade came over to Mandy's table one day at lunch and asked if they could sit with her. "Sure," she answered and scooted over to make room.

One of the two girls, Meredith, was new. Her father had moved to Seattle to work at Boeing, so they had something in common. The other girl, Sandy, had been there last year.

As they sat down, Sandy began to tell Meredith all about the quiz contest and how Mandy had won first place, just as though it had happened the day before. Mandy blushed, but it made her feel good that Sandy seemed to enjoy talking about it. She sounded as though she were proud to know Mandy.

From then on, the three spent time together at recess and during the lunch hour. And neither Meredith nor Sandy seemed to mind at all when Helga sat with them at lunch.

One day as they were eating together and joking about the lukewarm spaghetti, Mandy looked up to see Jane Stevens standing by the table. Jane looked as though she wanted to say something. Helga was sitting by Mandy's side, with Meredith and Sandy opposite them.

"Hello, Jane," Mandy said. "Want to sit down? There's room."

"Thanks, but I can't." She nodded toward the Golden Ring, sitting in another part of the cafeteria. "The others are expecting me to sit with them."

Mandy looked at her and waited a minute. "Did you need something?" she asked.

"I wanted to ask you a favor." Her voice was soft, as though she didn't want anyone to hear. "Mandy, do you think you could help me with my long division? I'm having a terrible time understanding it."

Before Mandy could answer, Helga spoke up. "Well, naturally she can help. Don't you remember who won the encyclopedia set last spring?"

To Mandy's surprise, Jane smiled. "I know she can, Helga. I'm asking if she will."

Helga chuckled. "She'll do that, too!"

Mandy nodded. "Helga's right. How about if we work on it tomorrow during library hour?"

"Swell. Thanks. See you then."

As Jane walked away, Mandy wondered if that was the first time Jane had ever talked to Helga in a civil tone.

Helga leaned over and said, "Don't look now, but the Golden Ring is getting a little tarnished."

The four girls burst into laughter.

CHAPTER 18

A Leader for the Future

The Mikimotos' small living room was jam-packed with McMichaels, crowded around the radio with their hosts to listen to the election returns.

Dad had been let off work early so he could vote. When he'd gotten home, he'd told Mama, "Call the Mikimotos. See if they want company this evening. We'll all listen to the returns together."

The Mikimotos were happy for their friends to drop by. Now they sat around eating, talking, and waiting for the news.

Just a week before the election, President Roosevelt had ordered the first peacetime military draft in the history of the United States. All eligible young men had signed up and been assigned numbers from 1 to 7,836. On the newsreel at the movies, Mandy saw Secretary of War Henry L. Stimson draw a number from the goldfish bowl that had been used during the Great War. He handed the number to President Roosevelt, and the president read out, "One hundred fifty-eight." All young men who had been assigned that number were now destined for boot camp.

Mandy looked over at Peter's young, handsome face smiling at some joke that Mr. Mikimoto had made, and she wondered if he would be marching off to war one day. She looked over at Lora, who seemed to have turned from a girl to a grown-up woman overnight as she worried about Mark's safety in the Philippines.

It was nearly midnight, and the twins were asleep—Susan on Dad's lap and Ben in a corner on the floor. Hideko and Caroline were in Hideko's bedroom listening to phonograph records.

Suddenly the news broke. Republican nominee Wendell Wilkie had conceded defeat. The entire room broke into a rousing cheer. Even quiet, demure Mrs. Mikimoto was cheering. They were waving their cups of tea and bottles of Coca-Cola in a rousing salute.

"Wait a minute," Peter said, waving his hand. "Wilkie's about to speak."

They instantly became quiet so they could listen to Mr. Wilkie's words.

"No matter which side you were on," came the defeated candidate's voice over the airwaves, "this great expression of faith in the free system of government must have given hope wherever man hopes to be free."

Then, referring to Mr. Roosevelt, Mr. Wilkie said, "He is your president. He is my president. And we will pray God may guide his hand during the next four years."

Mr. Mikimoto reached over and turned down the volume. "He is right. We must pray."

He bowed his head, and the others did the same. As Mandy listened to the prayer of this gentle, kind Japanese-American man, she, too, prayed for their president. And she prayed that God would equip him with the wisdom to guide their country through these perilous times.

OFFICIAL

SISTERS IN TIME

WEBSITE!

Your Adventure Doesn't Stop Here—

LOG ON AND ENJOY...

The Characters:
Get to know your favorite characters even better.

Fun Stuff:
Have fun solving puzzles, playing games, and getting stumped with trivia questions.

Learning More:
Improve your vocabulary and knowledge of history.

Plus you'll find links to other history sites, previews of upcoming *Sisters in Time* titles, and more.

Don't miss
www.SistersInTime.com!